THE

Also by Leo Kessler

The *SS Assault Regiment Wotan* Series

SS PANZER BATTALION
DEATH'S HEAD
CLAWS OF STEEL
GUNS AT CASSINO
THE DEVIL'S SHIELD
HAMMER OF THE GODS
FORCED MARCH
BLOOD AND ICE
THE SAND PANTHERS
COUNTER-ATTACK
PANZER HUNT
SLAUGHTER GROUND
HELLFIRE
FLASHPOINT
CAULDRON OF BLOOD
SCHIRMER'S HEADHUNTERS
WHORES OF WAR
SCHIRMER'S DEATH LEGION
SLAUGHTER AT SALERNO
MARCH OR DIE

The *Stormtroop* Series

STORMTROOP
BLOOD MOUNTAIN
VALLEY OF THE ASSASSINS
RED ASSAULT
HIMMLER'S GOLD
FIRE OVER KABUL
WAVE OF TERROR
EAGLES IN THE SNOW
FIRE OVER AFRICA

The *Otto Stahl* Series

OTTO'S PHONEY WAR
OTTO'S BLITZKRIEG!
OTTO AND THE REDS
OTTO AND THE YANKS
OTTO AND THE SS
OTTO AND THE HIMMLER LOVE LETTERS

LEO KESSLER

The Wolf Pack

Submarine 1

Futura

A Futura Book

First published in Great Britain in 1985
by Century Publishing Co Ltd

This Futura edition published in 1986

*All characters in this publication are fictitious
and any resemblance to real persons, living or dead,
is purely coincidental.*

ISBN 0 7088 2663 6

Printed and bound in Great Britain by
Collins, Glasgow

Futura Publications
A Division of
Macdonald & Co (Publishers) Ltd
Maxwell House
74 Worship Street
London EC2A 2EN

A BPCC plc Company

'We know no fear, comrades. Our motto is: Go in and sink.'
Admiral Doenitz, Head of the German U-Boat Service 1939

AUTHOR'S NOTE

The crane grunted and heaved under the strain. All of us standing on the beach tensed. Soon the tide would be coming in again and the promoters of the scheme would be forced to abandon it if the crane did not succeed now.

'Over six hundred Yanks they killed here that day,' one of the waiting reporters said. 'More than they did on Utah beach - and this was just *practising* for D-Day!'

I looked at my companion out of the corner of my eye. His English was good enough to understand what the reporter had said. What did it feel like to be the man who had killed over six hundred young men forty years before?

But his tough, lined old face revealed nothing. He kept his bright blue eyes firmly fixed on the crane struggling to lift the only tangible evidence of what he had done here that night.

Then there was a sudden cheer. The crane had done it! Slowly the Sherman - all thirty tons of it - started to emerge from the sea which had hidden it these forty years. Thc American tank was totally shell-encrusted and bright red with rust; the white star of the Invasion force on its turret was barely visible and its cannon was hanging and dripping with seaweed. Excitedly the reporters and photographers surged forward to take their pictures and we were left standing on the sands, shivering a little in the chill wind that raced across the Slapton Mere.

'April 28th 1944,' my companion said slowly . . . reflectively. 'We had a quarter moon and the sea was quite calm. I remember that quite clearly - and then we went in to sink them. *Los!*' he said in the tones of a man who was accustomed to giving orders - and having them obeyed. We started to plod back to the hotel higher up the cove where we were staying. 'Now,' he announced, 'I shall tell you my story.' He laughed a little harshly, eyes remembering other times. 'But I promise you, Herr Kessler, that it will not be a very pleasant one.'

Thus that day, forty years after the event that made him so famous (some would have said 'so infamous') *Kapitänleutnant* Christian Jungblut, the captain of the most celebrated German U-boat of all - the U-69 - started to tell his tale. As he had warned me, it was not a very pleasant one - not pleasant indeed!

So for the first time it is now possible to reveal the full story of Nazi Germany's greatest submarine ace: the one who outlived Prien, Kretschmer, Schepke and all the rest of the other aces. There had been no surrender for Commander Jungblut then. Not because he had been a fanatical Nazi, but because he had been devoted to his service and his crew. He had experienced the fear, the triumph, the waste and the final pathos of Germany's war. Now at last he began to tell that bitter tale of the U-69, Nazi Germany's feared *KILLER SUB* . . .

Leo Kessler Slapton, England
Kiel, Germany - Summer 1984

BOOK ONE

Sharks and Little Fishes

'The Navy my lad? It takes your life and gives you the world.'

[*Old German Naval Saying*]

CHAPTER 1

'*Scapa Flow, meine Herren*!' Captain Hanssen announced, as his officers gathered around him on the streaming, rocking conning-tower. 'The base of the greatest fleet in the world, the British Home Fleet!'

As one, his officers focused their night glasses, legs braced against the movement of the U-boat, and stared around the ring of black-grained sheets of rock rising up hundreds of metres from the heaving Atlantic, a few withered trees clinging to their summits like hunchbacked dwarfs.

Captain Hanssen gave them time. His mind was on other things, for he had been here before. As a fifteen-year-old midshipman he had sailed into these very same waters on that sad day so many years before when they had surrendered the German High Sea Fleet to the Tommies. Now twenty-one years later he was back and somewhere below him in the depths of the pounding Atlantic lay that same ship they had scuttled under the very noses of the surprised British.

'All right, gentlemen,' he broke the heavy brooding silence, punctuated by the hiss of the wind that blew across the great northern anchorage, 'there are three easily navigable entrances to Scapa Flow. Over there, Holm to the east, Hoxa to the south . . . and Hoy in the west.'

His officers followed him with their glasses, nodding their understanding, as they tried to penetrate the blacked-out harbour in which the enemy kept most of his warships this first month of the new war.

'Each of these entrances, according to Admiral Doenitz's* information, is guarded by a single line of *nets* - they look a bit like fisherman's lobster pots - which support another two-inch thick wire net.' Hanssen laughed harshly. 'And that net, *meine Herren*, is supposed to keep nasty people like ourselves out of Scapa Flow . . . Now how does the Tommy get his own ships in and out?' Hanssen answered his own question. 'He has gates. A length of floating net which is moved by two bar boats stationed on either side of it. That's the way ships are let in and out.'

'And that's the way we will go in, Captain!' *Leutnant* von Arco, his Number One, said eagerly, lowering his glasses.

Hanssen sniffed. Von Arco was one of the 'young turks', as the 'old salts' like himself called them: eagle-eyed fanatics who trotted out those fashionable new phrases like 'the Führer's eyes are upon us' and 'Our flag means more than death' at the drop of a hat. He didn't like them; and he didn't like von Arco in particular. 'Not *we*, Leutnant,' he corrected his Number One harshly, 'but *someone*!'

'But sir,' von Arco protested, his oilskins creaking as he threw up his arm as if he were about to salute his beloved Führer there and then, 'we're here. We've not been detected by the Tommies. What is to stop us from entering the Flow and letting them have a feel of our tin fish†? Heaven, arse and cloudburst, sir, we've been at war for over a month now and haven't notched up a single kill!'

'You'll have your fill of killing before it's all over, von Arco,' Hanssen said icily. 'Never fear, you - *or your next-of-kin* - will have a drawerful of tin‡ by the time this war finishes. Now no more talk. These are my orders. The Big Lion - Doenitz to you - has commanded me to pick one of these gates and put it under observation. We are to find out whether there is a controlled minefield in front of the net.

* Head of the German U-Boat Service
† Torpedoes
‡ Decorations for bravery

Further, how the small patrol vessels operate to protect the gate once it is opened. And finally,' Hanssen paused gravely, as if he had just realized himself the full implication of what he was about to say, 'we are to enter the gate and check whether there is a second net beyond the first.'

Someone gasped in the dripping darkness and young Ensign Doerr, the U-69's 'Moses',* whispered, '*Holy Strawsack, we're going in!*'

'That we are, Doerr,' Captain Hanssen agreed. 'Now let us not waste any more time. It will be first light in two hours time. Diving stations everyone, please!'

Von Arco, steely-eyed, back like a ramrod, not an ounce of superfluous fat on his trained body, stepped back from the periscope. '*Herr Kapitan*,' he barked as if he were back on the parade ground at Kiel-Wik, 'we are now at periscope depth!'

The bearded crewmen, busy at their instruments in the green-glowing, dripping interior of the submarine, which stank of oil, rancid food and human sweat, watched out of the corners of their eyes as the Captain prepared to have a first look at the gate at Hoy. Captain Hanssen was an old man for U-boat service, in his late thirties, with blue witty eyes in a lined, weather-beaten face. Now those same eyes sparkled with excitement as he turned his white cap back to front – on board ship he was the only one allowed to wear one – and approached the periscope. 'Periscope up!' he commanded in a matter-of-fact voice. Hanssen had long learned that it never did in the submarine service to show too much haste or excitement; it unsettled the younger men in the crew and that led to mistakes.

With a soft hiss, the gleaming steel tube went up. Hanssen pressed his face to the sight. Almost immediately the circle of calibrated glass cleared of water – and there it

* Nickname for the youngest member of a U-boat's crew

was: the broad expanse of Scapa Flow, packed with the enemy's capital ships. He didn't need the recognition charts to identify them. Their long grey shapes were as familiar to him as the faces of his own children. To port there was the *Royal Oak*; over there, that monster bristling with sixteen-inch guns was the *Warspite* and if he was not mistaken there was the aircraft carrier the *Ark Royal.* He licked his saltcaked lips suddenly, as if in anticipation of a great feast. God in heaven, it was a submarine captain's dream! The whole of the British Home Fleet at anchorage, there for the taking!

'Captain!' The look-out's tense voice cut into his reverie. 'Engines – zero forty degrees!'

'Stop engines!' Hanssen barked.

He swung the periscope round. Out of the grey dawn mist, a lean, rakish destroyer was heading for the gate. Behind it the little patrol boats zig-zagged back and forth, throwing up a furious wake of boiling white water. He spun the periscope round again. Slowly, to his front, the gate was being opened. The destroyer was going in, and the patrol boats which protected the entrance were *to his rear*!

Busy with their instruments as they were, his crew tensed, as if they already half-guessed what was going through the stocky little Captain's mind. Now above them the thunder of engines grew louder and louder. It was going to be now or never, they knew. Suddenly *Leutnant* von Arco blurted out what they all thought as they waited there in the green-glowing darkness, faces greased with sweat: 'Sir, are we going in?'

Hanssen made his decision, though he knew from the Old War that U-boat commanders who tried to sneak in through boom defences in the wake of a ship were usually dead U-boat commanders in short order. Yet the patrol boats *were* to his rear! He swallowed hard and rasped, 'Yes, we go in . . . Down periscope!'

Von Arco's eyes blazed and he gritted his brilliant-white

teeth, almost as if he were trying to suppress some overwhelming pain. '*My God, we're going in*!' he grated.

'Death Watch beetles!' Torpedo-Gunner's-Mate Frensen announced as the wooden panelling of the U-69 groaned and creaked under the pressure on her hull. He gave a big bearded smile, as if he enjoyed the alarming noise.

'Arse-with-ears!' his running-mate Torpedo-Rating Maydag snorted and wiped away the sweat with the ragged cloth that hung around his skinny neck. Like all sailors he was superstitious. 'You oughtn't to say things like that, Frensen. Painting the devil on the wall, it is!'

The big tough Hamburger tugged at the end of his bulbous nose, the product of years spent drinking *korn* and *kummel* in waterfront bars, and whispered, 'What's up, you little ape-turd? You scared because the skipper's taking us to see the nice Tommies?'

'Piss in the wind!' the wizened torpedo-rating snorted. 'It's just that you shouldn't –'

'Cut out that chatter back there!' Von Arco's harsh voice burst into the conversation. 'We're on silent running, remember!'

Frensen, the ex-communist docker who hated the Number One with a passion, made an obscene rubbing gesture with his clenched right fist. 'You know his trouble, don't yer?' he whispered out of the side of his mouth. 'He's just had an unhappy love affair. *He broke his right hand*!' But even the irrepressible Hamburger fell silent as the Captain twisted his white cap, the brass insignia green with verdigris, around his shaven skull and commanded softly, 'Periscope height, please.'

Nearby the hydrophone operator tensed over his instrument, following the sound of the Tommy destroyer's engines as they moved ever closer into the harbour.

The Skipper was going to check if they were through

the gate yet. Slowly, deliberately, Captain Hanssen approached the periscope and pressed his face to it. The crew tensed. This was the moment of truth. Those who could watched his back as if mesmerized. For what seemed an eternity, Hanssen crouched there. And then abruptly they could see his shoulders heaving, almost as if he were laughing to himself. He swung round, beckoning to Von Arco to have a look, and announced, his weathered face wreathed in a big tough smile, 'Boys we're through – and there isn't a second net in sight. *Scapa Flow is wide open*!'

CHAPTER 2

It was just before midday when the fog started to drift in from the Shetlands. At first it was nothing more than a few grey wisps, curling themselves softly and silently around the plodding old World War One destroyer flying the white ensign of the Royal Navy almost unnoticed. But slowly it thickened. It brought with it a freezing, bone-chilling, icy cold. On the exposed gun-platforms, the sailors did physical jerks in their heavy duffle coats and nailed sea-boots to keep warm. A couple waltzed together in mock solemnity. At the bows the look-outs leaned out over the rails, straining their eyes against that milky white wall. One of the cooks, peeling potatoes outside on deck, whistling 'Roll Out the Barrel', finally threw down his knife in anger, muttered, 'Fuck this for a tale,' and went inside. Everything sank slowly into the fog, bringing with it a brooding, chilling lethargy.

On the bridge, Lt. Commander Horseman, RNR, turned up his collar about his rugged crimson face and muttered pretty much the same crude expression before ordering the engine-room to reduce speed. The weather off Scapa Flow was bad enough as it was, without fog. How was he expected to patrol off this arsehole of the world in this kind of a pea-souper? Why in the devil's name had he ever volunteered to join the Royal Naval Reserve after retiring in '36? He ought to be at home down in Devon toasting his feet in front of a nice fire instead of freezing his balls off up here.

Now time passed leadenly, as the Captain steadily had the speed of the destroyer reduced. He ordered more look-outs. They ringed the ship, eyes narrowed against the freezing fog, ears straining for the slightest sound. Below, the specialist ratings crouched over their Asdic sets, faces glazed with sweat, earphones pressed to their ears, listening for a change in that regular *ping-ping-ping* which would indicate that an enemy submarine was lurking close by. All was icy, controlled tension.

The usually welcome cry of '*Rum-O*' signifying that every member of the crew over eighteen was entitled to receive half a mug of thick, brown, potent rum brought no relief this miserable fog-bound day. They were all on edge and too tense. Indeed, soon the magic warmth the rum brought had worn off and the crew slipped back into their freezing edginess. Now they began to see non-existent shapes and forms in the grey, billowing clouds of fog that locked them in on all sides, as the ancient destroyer wallowed through the swell. Twice look-outs called out false sightings only to have the Skipper's rage descend upon them in all its fury.

Now there was no sound save the pulsating throb of the destroyer's engines and the creak of her rigging as the ratings strained to penetrate that grey gloom. Like the Captain they were mostly reservists who had been recalled to duty in September 1939, but they all knew that if anything happened to their ship, they wouldn't live more than a few minutes in that sullen, freezing green water below.

Commander Horseman had just begun to indulge himself in a hot cup of cocoa, burying his frozen nose in the steam rising from the china mug, when it happened. '*Sub to port, sir*!' the excited cry of a look-out floated up from below.

Horseman dropped his mug with a crash. Next instant his binoculars flashed up. With fingers that trembled badly, he focused them. A lean, grey, devilish shape leapt into the circles of calibrated glass. There was no mistake. It was a submarine wallowing in a trough, half-submerged, *and it was a German*!

Horseman didn't hesitate. 'Port twenty,' he called, 'full ahead together!' Instinctively he braced himself for the shock. It came. As the helmsman wrenched round his wheel, the engines burst into full power. The destroyer's prow slammed into the waves, as her 30,000 horsepower engines thrust her forward, a great white bone in her teeth immediately. Horseman raised his voice against the sudden wind and yelled, 'Guns . . . stand by for surface action . . . Local control!'

Now Horseman's ship raced forward on a collision course, the U-boat still unaware, apparently, that it was being attacked. Below on the foredeck the gunners in their turrets tensed behind the four and a half-inch guns, gun-layers glued to their sights, sweating in spite of the cold. Behind them stood the rammers ready with their rods, while next to the breech the loaders in their flash-proof hoods and gloves waited, yellow-gleaming shells cradled in their brawny arms, ready to reload at a moment's notice. And on the bridge, Horseman, looking like a medieval man-at-arms in his flat helmet and white anti-flash hood, stood sucking his cold pipe, waiting for the joust to commence.

The pressure wave slapped von Arco across the face like a blow from a flabby, wet hand. A hollow boom. Next instant the sea to the left of the conning-tower boiled furiously. A great spout of churning, wild-white water hurtled upwards. Von Arco spun round, bearded face white with shock.

A long, lean, grey shape was racing through the fog straight at the U-69, scarlet flame stabbing from the narrow muzzles of its forward guns!

'*A Tommy*!' the look-out gasped next to him. '*A Tommy des* –' He screamed in absolute agony, as another shell exploded close to the submarine and the bridge was showered with red-hot metal and tons of icy water. He crumpled to the deck in a quivering heap, clutching his face with hands tightly pressed together through which bright-red blood seeped.

Desperately von Arco shouted, 'Clear the bridge . . . both engines emergency ahead . . . *alarrmmm*!'

Down below the sirens started to shriek. Men ran to their duty stations, pushing by each other in the narrow, stinking confines of the boat, cursing with rage and fear.

Again the forward turrets of the racing destroyer fired. There was a sound like a huge piece of canvas being ripped by a giant. Von Arco flung himself at the dripping hatch as the U-69 reeled under the shock wave, her rigging ripped to shreds by flying shrapnel. Desperately he clawed at the steel controls as water thundered down upon him in torrents, threatening to tear him from his perch. Then he was through, the hatch closed, falling in a soaked heap onto the deck at the Captain's feet.

But Captain Hanssen had no time for his shocked Number One. Now he knew he had only a matter of seconds left before the destroyer rammed him. He had only one course left. To dive to great depth and take the punishment that was going to come to him. Frantically he rapped out his orders. But the huge swells held the U-69 in their grasp. Struggle as the boat might to disappear beneath the waves, the surface tension held her as if in a sea of glue. 'All hands to the forward torpedo room!' Hanssen bellowed desperately. '*Dalli . . . dalli*!'

The free hands needed no urging. They knew the old trick the Skipper was attempting. Frantically they scrambled towards the front of the boat, past the hydrophone operator, his eyes bulging out of his head like those of a madman, as the noise of the enemy's screws grew ever louder in his ears.

Frensen and Maydag, dirty singlets wet and black with sweat, pressed themselves against the bulkhead as the swarm of ratings descended upon them. '*Come on, fuck you . . . come on*!' the big Hamburger yelled, fists doubled, face flushed with fury, as slowly, maddeningly slowly, the U-69 started to tilt downwards. '*Will you not fucking submerge – cow*!'

'*Stand by for depth charge attack*!' Hanssen yelled.

A roar. A crash. Someone screamed. For an instant the lights flickered then went out, leaving them in stinking, inky darkness. And then, as they came on again, they could feel they were going down. But still not fast enough. Another salvo of eight depth charges exploded all around the U-69. All the glass panels in the control room shattered. Suddenly the deck was strewn with gleaming splinters. The gyro-compass shot through the boat, whirling round at 10,000 revolutions per minute.

'Trim the boat for silent running,' Hanssen commanded, trying to keep himself from raising his voice, beads of sweat already hanging from his bushy eyebrows like glistening pearls. They still had not achieved any real depth and the Tommy directly above them was coming in for the kill. Already he could hear the enemy Asdic impulses hitting the U-boat's hull piercingly, threateningly, at regular intervals.

'Propellers at high speed, sir . . . Trying to pick us up on their Asdic, sir,' the harassed operator sang out, hands pressed to claws as he held on to his earphones as if his very life depended upon it.

Frensen looked at his running-mate, face now as pale as those of the others crowded into the torpedo compartment. 'Christ, Maydag!' he croaked, 'now the clock really is in the pisspot!'

Maydag nodded but said nothing, as if he didn't dare

speak in case his voice broke under the strain.

Von Arco looked at the Captain enquiringly, but Hanssen's tough face revealed nothing as he held onto a stanchion waiting for the next salvo of depth charges, eyes on the shattered instruments which told him nothing any more. Another handful of gravel, which was the enemy Asdic, hit the hull. A moment's silence. Two shattering blows. The whole boat shook crazily. Again the lights flickered and went out. Glass tinkled to the deck. 'Depth-gauge leaking, Captain,' von Arco reported, flashing on his torch to reveal the jet of icy water spurting into the control room.

'Thank you, Number One.' Hanssen managed to keep his voice under control - just.

The lights flashed back on again. Hanssen stared at the blank dials. Now they could no longer tell whether they were rising or sinking. His scalp crawled. What was he going to do?

'Propeller noise aft, sir,' the hydrophone operator sang out.

In the torpedo-compartment, the two running-mates Frensen and Maydag grabbed hastily for support, water already sloshing around their ankles. 'Now the friggers are gonna stick a salami up our asses!' Maydag snarled.

'*Ach*, knock it off,' the big Hamburger called back drawing himself up to his full height, almost as if he were preparing to die standing up like a man, 'all Tommies are four-eyed. They couldn't even hit your ass - and it's big enough!'

Captain Hanssen made up his mind. He knew there was no other alternative. He could either attempt to stick it out by diving to a depth impossible to gauge, or surface and fight to the finish. He knew he preferred to go down fighting rather than sweating out the last hours of his life slowly choking to death at the bottom of the ocean. 'Clear torpedo tubes one to five!' he commanded.

Frensen slammed a hand like a small steam-shovel down on Maydag's soaked, skinny shoulder joyfully, new hope in his eyes. 'Did you hear that, you little shiteheel? We're gonna fight it out. Now move it . . .'

Up in the control room, Hanssen turned to von Arco. 'All right Number One, I don't need to draw you a picture, do I? *Take her up*!'

CHAPTER 3

'*Torpedo – starboard*!' the look-out screamed frantically.

'*Hard to port*!' Captain Horseman yelled in a frenzy of apprehension, grabbing for support as the helmsman swung the wheel round. Out of the fog he could glimpse the frightening trail of bubbles racing straight for his ship. A moment later the deadly fish, laden with a ton of high explosive, hissed by the heeling destroyer with only feet to spare.

But the frantic RNR officer had not reckoned with the new tactics employed by the German U-boats. Suddenly torpedoes were racing towards the destroyer, fanning out in a wide arc so that it was virtually impossible to manoeuvre the ship out of the way.

Helplessly, mouth open almost stupidly, Lt. Commander Horseman waited for the inevitable. It came, even though the helmsman was zig-zagging furiously. There was a tremendous hollow boom followed almost immediately by another horrific hammer blow. The ship reeled violently. Its rigging seemed to touch the heaving water. Up the voice-tube came the eerie screaming of scalded, burned stokers and the sudden dread hiss of escaping steam. Abruptly the destroyer lost power and a shocked, mesmerized Horseman knew that his boiler room had been hit. He was without power.

Hanssen waited no longer. 'Down periscope!' he barked,

even while the torpedo-men were still cheering their success. 'Take her up. Gun crew stand by!'

'Gun crew up forrad!' von Arco commanded. As Number One, he was also torpedo and artillery officer.

The men tumbled forward, already clad in their oilskins. 'Up periscope,' Hanssen ordered once more, knowing what a devil of a risk he was taking. The destroyer might well be crippled, but she still had teeth and he had a lot of respect for the Tommies of the Royal Navy; they'd fight to the end, and he had only four torpedoes left.

Gently he inched the periscope upwards, the sweat trickling down the small of his back. He had to spot the position of the enemy ship without giving his own away – yet. Goddam that shattered depth gauge! This was like feeling your way around a pitch-black room with your hands cased in boxing gloves. Suddenly he caught his breath. The rushing water had fled from the streaming circle of glass. There she was. The Tommy destroyer, thick, black, oily smoke pouring from a fire midships, obviously drifting and out of control. He licked suddenly parched lips, wrinkling his face at the taste of the salt which caked them permanently when he was at sea. This was it.

'All right, Number One.' He managed to control his voice with difficulty. 'I'll give you exactly thirty seconds. I want you and your men topside in that time.'

'You can rely on me, sir!' von Arco replied, face fanatical and vain.

'Torpedo-men stand by!' Hanssen cried.

'Standing by, sir!' Frensen called, crouched over his tubes, face glazed with sweat, his brutally muscled shoulders tensed.

'*Now*!' Hanssen yelled.

Suddenly they had broken the surface. Icy-cold air came streaming in. Men clattered up the dripping ladder. In the very same instant that the destroyer's four and a half-inch guns thundered into action once more, von Arco and his crew were pelting across the dangerously slick deck towards the sole 88mm cannon there.

Up above, the conning-tower machine-gun chattered frantically. Cartridge cases, steaming furiously, came clattering down in a mad, yellow rain. Hanssen ignored them. Desperately he swung the submarine round so that he presented the smallest possible target to the enemy. A salvo of shells landed close by. The U-69 heeled madly, as if struck by a sudden tornado. Suddenly the machine-gunner screamed shrilly and came clattering down the tower to sprawl dead at the Captain's feet. A free hand sprang over the shrapnel-ridden body to scramble up the ladder and take over the gun. The gun burst into life once more.

'Hein!' Hanssen shouted to the engineer-officer. 'Take the con!'

Hurriedly the small, rotund engineer took over the controls. Madly Hanssen scrambled up the ladder to view the scene for himself. Further up the deck, von Arco had almost got the 88mm into action. There was no time to lose. The drifting destroyer was less than five hundred metres away, and although she could only bring her aft gun turret to bear, the Tommy gunners were laying down a furious barrage. All around the U-69 the water boiled and heaved with near misses, while the enemy machine-gunners peppered the length of the submarine. It could be only a matter of minutes, perhaps seconds, before the Tommy gunners got lucky. At this range, they couldn't miss.

He slid down the ladder at speed, ignoring the burning sensation in his hands just as the 88mm opened up with a tremendous roar. The last stage of the battle had commenced.

Horseman ducked as white zig-zagging lines of tracer

streaked towards the drifting ship, growing in speed by the instant. Slugs ripped the length of the destroyer with a sound like a metal rod being run along a line of iron railings. Holes appeared everywhere. The deck splintered. Rigging tumbled down. A seaman screamed hysterically and reeled back from his machine-gun, what looked like a series of red buttonholes stitched suddenly across his chest. '*Damn . . . damn . . . damn*!' Horseman cursed, overwhelmed with anger at his own impotence. If only he had power and rudder, he'd ram the German. But he didn't.

Aft the sweating gunners fired another salvo and the Germans grouped around their 88mm cannon seemed to fall apart, abruptly a mass of flailing arms and legs in the sudden ball of angry fire. '*Bull's-eye*!' a rating cried wildly before going down in a heap the next moment as a burst of German machine-gun fire caught him. A radio mast fell on top of him a second later and his dead body twitched and writhed in the blue-flashing, fiery-sparked metallic spider's web.

Beyond himself with anger and despair, Horseman dropped from the riddled bridge to where the dead man lay slumped, dripping blood over his machine-gun. He thrust him to one side and took up the firing position, the butt of the ancient Lewis gun tucked into his shoulder. He pressed the trigger. The machine-gun chattered into furious activity. Tracer began to howl off the conning-tower of the U-boat. Suddenly he was overcome by a feeling of great satisfaction. For what it was worth he was fighting back. But not for long.

The last of Hanssen's torpedoes caught the British completely by surprise. Not even the aft look-out, who died in the same instant that it slammed into the ship's aft with a hellish thud, saw it as the whole ship reeled and heeled under that massive impact. The rest of the superstructure came tumbling down in a mess of rending metal and wire.

Men screamed in unbearable pain as they were trapped by the falling burning debris. Others sank to their knees, hands clutching their throats as they choked on the acrid fumes. Some simply died where they stood, not a mark on their bodies, their lungs ripped apart by the awesome blast. Rapidly the shattered destroyer began to sink . . .

'*Hurrah . . . hurrah . . !*' the crew cheered, wild with excitement as the Captain made his announcement and clattered up the ladder once again to view the dying enemy.

The destroyer presented an indescribable mess. All was twisted, grotesquely torn metal, mixed up with bits and pieces of equipment, as desperate men ran across the bodies of the dead on the sloping deck, throwing Carley floats over the side into the churning sea, or attempted to hack the lifeboats free with their axes. Here and there English sailors, hysterical with fear, had thrown themselves overboard into the icy water and were swimming furiously with the last of their strength. For now the destroyer, littered everywhere with the pathetic debris of a dying ship, was readying itself for its last plunge to the bottom of the sea.

Von Arco clattered up the turret. His eyes were filled with hatred. Blood streaked the side of his arrogant face; more dripped from his wounded hand. 'Beg to report deck-88 knocked out, sir.'

Hanssen frowned. 'Casualties?' he asked, not taking his eyes off the awesome spectacle of the dying destroyer. Somewhere a ship's whistle was shrilling mournfully now like the keening of some eerie banshee.

'The whole crew, sir. I was lucky.' Suddenly von Arco's savage rage broke through. He darted across the tower and before Hanssen could stop him he had seized the machine-gun from the surprised rating and was firing wildly into the swimming men, racing the chattering weapon from side to side, slaughtering the survivors mercilessly.

'In God's name!' Hanssen cried. He grabbed hold of von Arco and heaved him from the gun, sending a wild burst of white tracer zig-zagging harmlessly into the fog. '*What do you think you are doing, man?*'

Von Arco swung round on him, his eyes mad with fury. 'They killed our men! We must kill them!' he blurted out, his chest heaving with rage as if he had just run a great race. 'In this war, there must be no mercy shown. The New Germany does not indulge itself in Jewish sentimentality!' He spat the words into Hanssen's face defiantly, as if he was challenging the Captain to say the contrary. 'Besides, witnesses would endanger our mission.'

'*Damn the mission, Leutnant von Arco*!' Captain Hanssen bellowed at the top of his voice as if he were back on the bridge of the windjammer he had trained on as a kid. 'No man in my crew is going to shoot helpless sailors in the water, even if they are the enemy. Consider yourself under open arrest. Now go below and work out a quick course so that I can give it to those poor fellows.'

For one long moment it almost seemed as if an enraged *Leutnant* von Arco would refuse to obey the Captain's order as he towered above Hanssen, fists clenched in rage. Then suddenly he turned and clattered down the ladder without another word.

Five minutes later the U-69 was on its way again, limping into the thick white fog, leaving behind a handful of survivors bobbing up and down on the waves among the debris and the dead, staring after it as if they were just witnessing the passing of a ghost . . .

CHAPTER 4

The new First Sea Lord raised himself from his bath, removed the big cigar from his mouth, popped in his bottom and top plates which were handily situated at the side of the tub next to the glass of brandy and cried, 'Enter, pray!'

Payne entered, the usual folder under his arm, the usual solemn look on his bland civil servant's face. Often, the First Sea Lord told himself, slightly amused at his assistant, he could have sworn the man had lemonade in his veins and not blood.

'Well?' he demanded, taking a defiant sip of his brandy, just to anger Payne (though he wondered if Payne had ever experienced such an emotion, or any emotion for that matter). For it was only ten in the morning and he knew drinking at this hour would definitely irritate his assistant.

But if it did, Payne's face revealed nothing as he came to a halt in front of the bath, tugged at his black jacket and tried not to look too directly at his new master who wallowed there in the suds like a pink Buddha. 'Sir,' he said solemnly, 'I have news.'

'Then pray,' the First Sea Lord waved his cigar as if he were conducting an invisible orchestra, 'as our American cousins would say - spill it!'

'HMS *Hardy* has been torpedoed, sir, off the Shetlands . . . and sunk,' Payne announced, his voice totally without emotion.

The First Sea Lord frowned. All his life he had been

accustomed to sending men on missions from which they might well not return, but still, all these years later, he could not become accustomed to losses. 'Many casualties?' he asked hesitantly.

'About one hundred, sir. They have taken the survivors to Scapa. The Captain was badly wounded. He's in the *Saint Abba*.'

'The hospital ship?'

'Yessir.'

'Could he give any details?'

'Yessir.' Payne consulted his notes. 'He was attacked by a surfaced U-boat, which received some considerable punishment. But in the end the U-Boat managed to put his steering mechanism out of order and then the German torpedoed him. There was some indiscriminate firing at the survivors in the water, but the German captain soon put a stop to it and gave the survivors a course to steer for home.'

The First Sea Lord nodded his bald, domed head, as if in silent approval, and took a slow reflective sip of his brandy, while Payne watched in silent wonder. What other minister would receive his staff naked in his bath, sipping brandy, at ten o'clock in the morning, he asked himself. But then the First Sea Lord was no ordinary minister. Even the Royal Navy's hard-bitten captains and admirals had cheered when the Prime Minister had announced in the Commons who the new First Sea Lord was going to be, a month ago.

The man in the bath put down his glass. 'Be so kind as to hand me a towel, Payne.'

Hastily the civil servant complied and the First Sea Lord stepped naked out of his bath and with the towel draped about his plump, hairless body and trailing water behind him, he paddled into his study, already fumbling for his spectacles. He peered thoughtfully at the big map of the British Isles attached to the far wall and said softly, almost as if he were speaking to himself, 'Sad . . . sad . . . sad . . .'

Payne coughed discreetly into his fist and wondered whether he should tell the great man that his fat buttocks were visible beneath the towel, but decided against it. He waited, notebook at the ready.

'Years of neglect,' the First Sea Lord growled. 'Years of neglect! The Flow is defended worse than it was in World War One. No coastal batteries. The indicator net and minefield removed in 1918. Only eight anti-aircraft guns available to defend the whole anchorage.' He shook his bald head sadly. 'What guilty men have ruled our destinies in these last years! Now we are faced with the greatest air-striking power the world has known and only eight guns to defend the whole of the Home Fleet!'

Payne thought it was time to say something. After all, he knew ministers of old; they expected to be fed leading questions at regular intervals. 'Do you think this lone submarine was watching Scapa Flow, sir?' he asked.

For a moment the First Sea Lord did not reply. Instead he gazed out of the window at the barrage balloons floating above Whitehall like fat grey slugs. Finally he said, 'Yes. The Hun is going to attack the place with his damned *Luftwaffe*, I am sure of it. The Hun is not attempting to take aerial photographs of the Flow because he does not want to alert us. So he sends a sub. Even with the poor defences we have, no sub could penetrate the anchorage, so it must be that they are intending to make an aerial attack.' He stared at Payne as if he were seeing his bland civil servant's face for the very first time. 'Make a signal to Flag-Officer-Commanding, Home Fleet.' Hastily Payne scribbled down the words. 'Order Home Fleet to disperse to other Scottish bases. Action this day.'

Payne looked up. 'Sir, the *Royal Oak*? You know how slow she is. She would be a considerable burden to Admiral Forbes*.'

* Commander-in-Chief of the Home Fleet

The First Sea Lord nodded his bald head in agreement. 'You are right. Add to the signal that the *Royal Oak* should stay behind. She will act as a floating anti-aircraft battery in the Flow's defensive scheme. Now hurry that off and pass me my brandy - fill it up before you go.'

'Yes sir,' Payne said and carried out the First Sea Lord's orders. A moment later he was gone, leaving the great man still draped only in the wet towel, glass in hand, staring out at a Whitehall dripping with a sad, cold rain, alone with his thoughts. It was ten-fifteen on the morning of September 30th 1939 and the First Sea Lord, Winston Churchill, had just saved the British Home Fleet, but, unwittingly, had also condemned twelve hundred British sailors to a terrible death . . .

Five hundred miles away from where Winston Churchill made his fateful decision that wet morning in London, the sailor who would bring about that terrible execution also brooded, alone with his thoughts. Outside in the fiord, the tugs tooted their whistles merrily and on the barracks square a petty officer, voice thickened with years of Schnaps, was bellowing at the squad of recruits: 'What's the matter with you bunch of shitting wettails? Have you all got two shitting left feet?'

Commodore Karl Doenitz heard neither the tug whistles nor the coarse shouts. His cold blue eyes were fixed on that sparkling stretch of icy-green water, as if he were visibly willing the missing U-69 to come sailing up, the victory pennants fluttering from its conning-tower. It was now over twenty-four hours since they had picked up the faint signal announcing that Captain Hanssen had sunk an enemy destroyer: a signal which had been confirmed by this morning's BBC news. Since then nothing had been heard of Hanssen.

Doenitz frowned, his flat face that looked as if it had

been carved from granite cracking into deep, severe lines. It was vital to his plan that he have the information Hanssen could provide. The war in Poland was over and as yet the *Kriegsmarine*,* especially the U-boat arm, had played absolutely no role whatsoever in the fighting. It was imperative that he prove to the Führer that his submarines were the most powerful weapons in Germany's possession. The Führer was a 'land-rat'. He did not realize that the one and only way to bring a maritime island power like Britain to its knees was to starve it out; and his U-boats were the only weapon that could do that. The days of capital ships were over. But he knew Adolf Hitler. He, Doenitz, could only gain the Führer's ear if he pulled off that grand coup that he had been planning for all these years. Suddenly, angrily, Doenitz slammed his clenched fist down on his desk, its sole decoration that model of the old-fashioned World War One submarine which he had once commanded himself. *Where in three devils' name was the U-69?*

There was a tap at the door and Neurath, his Adjutant, thrust his head around the door. 'Sir,' he said.

'Yes?' Doenitz sat up expectantly, blue eyes hard and fanatical. 'Hanssen?'

Neurath shook his sleek black head. 'No sir. It's the ensigns, sir. They're coming in now, sir. I know you would want to say a few words to them before they go to their quarters.'

Doenitz forgot the U-69. 'Yes, yes, Neurath. Of course.' He picked up his cap and grey gloves. 'Have them paraded. I shall address them in five minutes.'

Ensign Christian Jungblut took a deep, grateful breath of the damp sea air, heavy with the odour of tar, salt and oil

* The German Navy

mingled with the smell of fish, seaweed and paint, and stared around at the naval barracks. Three years ago he and his fellow ensigns, waiting to be addressed by Doenitz, had taken their exams here as seventeen-year-olds. Now, after three years of hard training, they were going to the front at last. This day they would be given their assignments and allotted to their ships. At last the war, with its promise of excitement, adventure - and glory - could begin for him. In spite of his tiredness from the long monotonous train journey right across Germany from Koenigsberg, he felt a thrill of anticipation begin to surge through his long, lean body.

Three long years it had taken. An eternity of classes, drills, seaborne schools and sheer, relentless misery at the hands of tough old petty officers and supercilious, arrogant officer-instructors. Now his youth had vanished. Security was behind him. His family, so far away in that nice, safe Black Forest village, was forgotten. Now there would be action, women, medals - perhaps death. But what did it matter? He was going to war at last. Instinctively Christian Jungblut's fingers sought his cap and tilted it at a more rakish angle on his blond head. How long would it take, he wondered, before he won his first medal?

'*Stillgestanden*!' the arrogant-looking Adjutant barked harshly.

As one, twenty pairs of shoes stamped to attention, sending the gulls off in flight, cawing in hoarse protest.

Neurath swung round and marched back to the platform where Doenitz stood, the white and black flag of the *Kriegsmarine* fluttering above him in the stiff North Sea breeze. 'New ensigns all present and correct, *sir*!' he reported at the top of his voice.

Next to Jungblut, Fat Gierek whispered out of the side of his mouth, 'Hasn't he got a lovely arse!'

'Shut it!' Christian hissed, 'The Old Man is going to speak.'

But Doenitz took his time. Standing there, tall, skinny and poker-faced, he stared around at the circle of new arrivals with those icy blue eyes of his, as if he wished to impress each individual's features on his mind for ever. They waited.

Suddenly he started talking, the words flowing from his mouth in short, harsh phrases as if his jaw were worked by steel springs. '*Kameraden*, I need not tell you the victories our comrades of the *Luftwaffe* and Army have achieved in Poland. Radio and press have made much of them. Perhaps too much.' Doenitz frowned. 'But what have we done? The man in the street is saying, "The boys in blue are sitting on their sailor arses, twiddling their thumbs, while the Army and Air Force do all the fighting".' Doenitz brought his gloved fist down hard, almost as if he were striking someone. 'It has got to end!' he barked, his breath fogging on the icy air.

Christian Jungblut was impressed. The 'Big Lion', as the men called Doenitz behind his back, was a fighter, that was certain. He would ensure that his subs wouldn't be bottled up in their harbours, as was the case with the big ships at Admiral Raeder's* command. For whatever reason, Doenitz would send his U-boat fleet to battle – and damn the cost in men and material!

'Soon, you young ensigns will be going into battle – take my word for it, you will!' the Big Lion continued in that same harsh manner. 'The time has come to prove yourselves. You *will* take on the Tommies wherever you find their ships!' The Big Lion stabbed the air with his gloved hand. 'You *will* break their power at sea! You *will* bring them down to their knees! *You will win victory*!' Doenitz paused for breath, eyes glistening fanatically.

Next to Jungblut, Fat Gierek shivered. 'What's up?' Jungblut asked. 'Louse run over your liver?'

* Commander-in-Chief of the German Navy

'Yes, a whole shitting herd of them!' Gierek whispered back. 'That Big Lion certainly puts the shits up Frau Gierek's handsome and well-nourished son.'

Jungblut smiled to himself.

Doenitz began to wind up his little speech, borrowing from the hated Tommies, who had once been his captors in the Old War, Nelson's classic phrase: '*Meine Herren*, this day Germany expects every man to do his duty.' For one long moment he let those famous words ring in their ears, then he touched his gloved hand to his cap as if in salute. 'Dismiss the officers, *Herr Oberleutnant*,' he commanded Neurath.

The arrogant-looking lieutenant clicked to attention and swung round to face the rigid young ensigns standing there in the middle of that wind-swept barracks square. 'You will now dismiss to the supply and command ship *Lech*, where you will receive your orders. *Dis-miss*!'

As one, they saluted and started marching smartly towards the gate and the Tirpitz Pier beyond, leaving Doenitz standing there under that fluttering black and white flag, staring after them as if he did not expect to see many of them again . . .

CHAPTER 5

'Aircraft – *alaaarm*!' The shout of alarm died abruptly on Ensign Doerr's lips. The front of his uniform seemed to bubble strangely. In front of Maydag's horrified gaze, the Ensign's knees began to buckle beneath him like those of a newborn foal. With startling suddenness a scarlet jet of blood shot from his open mouth and soaked Maydag's terror-stricken face.

Frensen, the third member of the conning-tower watch, ducked instinctively as the plane swept across the boat, dragging its evil black shadow behind it. Next moment the bombs exploded – *one*, *two*, *three*, *four* – in a furious spout of whirling water and he was crying, '*Sunderland attacking . . . Sunderland attacking*!' while Maydag threw the dead Ensign into the interior of the boat, loud with the shrill, dread warning of the klaxon.

A haggard, red-eyed Hanssen could have groaned out loud at the sight of the dead officer, his back ripped open by that cruel surprise burst. Instead he called, trying to keep his voice calm, 'Dive . . . dive . . . dive . . !'

Madly the operators whirled their planes, showering Maydag and Frensen with icy sea-water as they dropped to the deck, and von Arco tried his best to judge the depth without the benefit of depth gauges. This was their third air attack in the last twelve hours and Hanssen knew that there would be more before they reached the safety of the German air defences. For now they were passing through those narrow straits between Denmark and Germany which led into the Baltic. Here the Tommies would not hesitate to violate the neutral Danes' airspace to attack this tempting target; they would go all-out to sink the U-69, already so badly damaged. God in heaven, if only his radio would work! He'd soon have the *Luftwaffe* scrambling to knock the Tommy shits out of the sky!

'What depth do you think we are, Number One?' Hanssen asked, as von Arco counted the seconds off silently. 'My guess is roughly seventy-five metres, Captain,' von Arco answered swiftly and hurried on counting.

'Then let's take her down to –' An ear-shattering boom. Like a gigantic steel fist, the detonation slammed against the side of the U-69. A spread of bombs lifted the boat clean out of the water, leaving her on the surface, her screws churning helplessly. For some seconds there was a loud-echoing silence, while the Captain stared helplessly at von Arco. *What were the Tommies, presented with this perfect target, going to do now?*

They did nothing! Perhaps they were baffled as they hovered there, staring at the suddenly reappeared U-boat. Then abruptly, after what seemed an eternity of waiting, the U-69 sank beneath the waves and once more the bombs came raining down.

Now as they limped ever closer to the entrance of the Baltic and safety, the Sunderland flying boats attacked them in swarms, relentlessly, bitterly determined to knock out this tin fish below the heaving, boiling water and send it to the bottom of the North Sea for good.

Time after time they came winging in to drop their deadly eggs. The battered U-69 was already listing badly. Everywhere she was leaking. The aft bilge was full of water. The white-faced, sweat-glazed crew, eyes bulging from their heads like those of the demented, were already up to their ankles with it, and Hanssen knew the more water he took on board the more chance he had, due to the extra weight, of plunging to the bottom – for good. 'We're caught between the shitting devil and the shitting blue sea, von Arco!' he explained grimly, wiping the sweat from his furrowed brow with the back of his hand. 'If we go up, the Tommies will land one of their square eggs on top of us. If we ship more water . . .' He spread his hands eloquently and left the rest of his sentence unfinished.

Von Arco, now frankly frightened and no longer posturing for once, nodded his agreement. He knew what the Captain meant. 'But what can we do, sir – surrender?'

Hanssen looked at him aghast. '*Surrender*, did you say, Number One? *Himmelherrgott*, you must be out of your mind! I'd rather go down with the ship than surrender her. No, by God, no!' He bit his bottom lip, his mouth suddenly full of the salt that caked it. 'We've got to trick them somehow.' He turned to the chubby little engineer-officer. 'How are we fixed for compressed air?' he asked.

Another pattern of bombs racked the boat and the engineer was nearly torn off his feet. The U-69's list became even more alarming. Time was running out – fast. 'Enough, sir,' the fat engineer quavered, the naked fear in his voice all too clear.

'Good,' Hanssen snapped, the trick forming rapidly in his mind. He turned and looked up the boat to the forward torpedo room. 'You up there, you, Fransen, you horned-ox, and that little turd of a pal of yours, Maydag.'

Frensen's big tough face broke into a grin. The skipper was putting up a tremendous show in spite of the miserable situation in which they found themselves.

'Get the duds off, shoes and all. Come on, at the double. And into Number Two tube with them. It's empty. *Los* . . !'

Frensen giggled in a high falsetto as he ripped the dirty singlet from his muscular body. 'And none of you naughty men are to look when I take off my lace drawers, mind you.' Swiftly Maydag and Frensen tore off their few clothes and stuffed them in the tube as the Captain had ordered.

Hanssen waited impatiently, dreading the next explosion, for it might well signify their end. 'Right then,' he ordered the engineer-officer when they were finished and both standing naked over the tube, faces now tense and businesslike, waiting for the Captain's order, 'Expel air from the outboard valve!'

Suddenly the crew understood. The Skipper was going to fake a sinking. New hope leapt into their worn, red-rimmed eyes. Here and there a rating whispered to himself, '*Toi . . . toi . . . toi.*'*

The fat engineer leapt to carry out the Skipper's command. There was the sudden hiss of escaping air. Silently Hanssen counted off the seconds he estimated it would take the air to reach the surface and explode there in great obscene bubbles to be dragged away immediately by the current and fool the Tommies.

'Now,' he yelled, 'fire Two!'

Frensen didn't hesitate. He pulled the trigger, the heavy muscles rippling along the length of his back. Their clothes shot to the surface to follow the bubbles.

Suddenly Hanssen leaned back against the periscope tube, all energy drained from his body, as if someone had just opened a tap. Now there was nothing more he could do but wait . . . *and pray* . . .

Commander Hanssen looked at his watch for the umpteenth time. It was now two hours since they had sent up their decoy. Already their oxygen was running out and now the men squatted in the dim light (the lighting had been turned off to conserve energy for their electric motors), breathing through the hot cartridges pressed to their mouths,† bodies stiff with cold, stress and fear.

* The German equivalent of crossing one's fingers for luck

† Device used to purify the stale air, heavy with carbon monoxide

Hanssen took the cartridge away from his mouth for a moment and his nostrils were immediately assailed by the stench of waste, sweat, oil and the gas escaping from the leaking batteries. His heart went out to his young sailors as they bent there numbly, their uniforms soaked with the cold water dripping from the pipes and the bulkheads. Had they realized what they were letting themselves in for when they had volunteered for the Submarine Service? He coughed thickly and realized it was time to put on his potash cartridge once more. He slipped the rubber tube leading to the metal box on his chest into his mouth again and took a deep gulp of the warmed, semi-purified air that came through it. It was foul, but it was better than choking to death.

Time passed leadenly. Here and there he could see young sailors nodding off, as if they were going to take a nap, only to be shaken awake immediately by their neighbours; for from that particular sleep there would be no more awakening. Others played with their fingers, writhing them in and out as if their nerves were stretched to breaking point and it would not be long before they ripped off their masks and burst out screaming. Even Frensen, that big ape of a torpedo-mate, stared dully and emotionlessly at the water dripping off the bulkhead, like a man who had given up all hope.

Hanssen looked at his watch yet once again. It was three hours since they had submerged, and in that time they had not been attacked. He'd have to take a chance that the Tommies had flown away. Soon it would be dark anyway. With the last of his strength he pulled the tube out of his mouth and nodded to the fat little engineer. 'All right, Hein, take her up!' he commanded, his voice harsh and rasping.

The engineer hesitated only an instant. Then he set to work. Using the last of their compressed air and electric battery power, he began to bring the U-69 up, while the crew, still wearing their masks, tensed at their duty stations, sweat trickling down their foreheads. Metre by metre they moved upwards. Then suddenly the sub started to move fast. Hein let her have her head, as if she were a live thing with a mind of her own. 'Boat rises fast!' he called.

'About fifty metres!' von Arco cried.

'Rising faster!'

'Twenty metres!'

'*Surfaced!*' Hein yelled.

Hanssen, breathing hard and fast like an ancient asthmatic in the throes of a fatal attack, waited no longer. He forced himself up the ladder and opened the hatches. Blessed fresh air streamed in. For a moment Hanssen almost fainted with the impact of that blessed, oxygen-rich air. He went down onto his knees in the conning-tower, shaking his head like a boxer trying to avoid going down for the count. Red and silver stars exploded in front of his eyes. There was a great black roaring in his ears.

Below, the men ripped the masks from their ashen, haggard faces and took great gulps of the cold sea air, hands on hips, heads tilted upwards like athletes.

Hanssen fought off his faintness. He raised himself with the help of a stanchion and stared to left and right across the darkening sea. The sky was empty in every direction. The Tommies had gone; they had given up! 'Both diesels half ahead,' he called down, as von Arco clattered up the ladder to survey the area too. 'Steer one-eighty. Ventilate the boat . . . Secure for action stations . . .'

New energy surged through the crew as more and more blessed air rushed in through the ventilators. The electric motors used for driving the U-69 below the surface were switched off. The diesels coughed into throaty life. Slowly the submarine started to move off once again, while Hanssen stood on the conning-tower bridge surveying the shattered superstructure, the red paint showing through everywhere where the bombs had struck like the symptoms of some loathsome skin disease. It had been nip-and-tuck all right. A very narrow escape indeed.

He put his head inside once more and called, 'Any noise, soundman?'

'No sir,' the operator called back happily as he crouched over his instrument.

Hanssen nodded his thanks and, turning to von Arco, said happily, 'Well, Number One, if we can achieve some sort of normal surface running speed, we should make . . .' He stopped suddenly. Von Arco was not listening. Instead his eyes were fixed hypnotically on the dark-green water to port. 'What is it, Number One?' he demanded somewhat sharply.

'Look over there, sir,' von Arco answered. 'Am I mistaken?' he asked wretchedly. 'The light's so damned bad. But isn't . . . isn't that . . . *a mine over there*?'

Commander Hanssen's heart sank. The Tommies might have been fooled, but they had played safe. In the three hours that the U-69 had been under the sea, they had whistled up their mine-laying planes. Now to reach safety his poor battered boat and harassed crew would have to sail through an uncharted minefield – *in the dark*!

CHAPTER 6

The room was filled with officers of all ranks. Most of them wore snow-white jackets and to Christian Jungblut they looked very relaxed and pleased with themselves as the stewards circulated, handing out drinks from silver trays. But then he supposed, as he stood in the corner with the rest of the new ensigns, they had good reason to be. This was the ideal life for a naval officer. He lived and worked on a ship, saw the water all day, but at night he could enjoy what pleasures Kiel had to offer. In the big old depot ship, an officer could spend the whole war in luxury and never hear a single shot fired in anger.

'Typical lot of rear-echelon stallions, what, Christian?' Fat Gierek exclaimed and looked longingly at the glass of foaming beer that one of the immaculate stewards was pouring for a paymaster-commander. 'Live like God in France in this old tub, they do.'

'Not pigging it like rough, tough old front-swine like ourselves, eh?' Jungblut pulled his fat companion's leg.

'Well, we are going to the front, aren't we?' Gierek protested. 'We're the ones who are going to pull *their* chestnuts out of the fire for them while they live in luxury on the *Lech*!'

Jungblut grunted and slipped back into his own thoughts, wondering what his particular assignment would be. Now they had been waiting for over an hour for Neurath to make an appearance and soon it would be lunch and they would have to clear the ward-room. Where in three devils' name was that arrogant bastard, with his overlong, sleeked dark hair and his haughty face which seemed always to look as if he had just smelled something very unpleasant? Nervously the handsome young ensign lit yet another cigarette and continued to wait.

It was eleven o'clock when Neurath, who had also changed into a snow-white jacket, finally made his appearance and waved them to follow him into the corner, away from the other officers, a handful of papers in his elegantly manicured hand. Hastily the ensigns formed a circle around him, nervously drawing on their cigarettes as they waited for their fates to be announced.

Neurath took his time, enjoying his power over them. Out of the side of his mouth Fat Gierek whispered contemptuously, 'He looks as if he's been bitten by a sick monkey, the pompous swine!'

At last Neurath began to speak. One by one he called the ensigns' names and told them which boat they had been assigned to and where it was stationed. Suddenly the class of crewmates were being posted all over Germany – Bremerhaven, Danzig, Koenigsberg. Waiting anxiously for his own name to be called, Christian Jungblut realized abruptly that this was the end of the road for the Class of '37; it was the parting of the ways. One by one his old comrades clicked their heels and accepted their orders, ready to race off and get their passes, permits, travel orders and the like from the paymaster's office. Yet his name obstinately refused to appear out of the conjuror's hat.

Finally the Adjutant was finished. 'That is it, *meine Herren*. There is no time for idle talk. Shake hands and get on your way. After all, in case you have forgotten it,' his mouth twisted in a crooked smile, 'there is a war on, you know.'

Jungblut looked at him in bewilderment. 'But me, sir,' he stuttered. 'I have not received my assignment yet!'

Neurath stared at him as if he had just crawled out of the

woodwork. 'You, Ensign, will remain aboard the depot ship,' he said arrogantly.

Christian Jungblut felt his cheeks flush. He was stunned. 'But what can I do here, sir?' he protested.

Neurath looked at him disdainfully. 'You can play my general dogsbody, office-boy sort of thing. But if it gives you any satisfaction, I can tell you that you have been given an assignment. It is to the U-69.' He gave a polite titter. 'What a curious number? No matter. That is your ship.'

'But where is she, sir?' Jungblut persisted.

'Where?' Neurath pretended to consider. 'Well, my guess is that *she's at the bottom of the North Sea*!'

With that he was gone, leaving Christian Jungblut blindly shaking the hands of his departing comrades, already aware of the gulf between them and him. For now he had become a 'rear echelon stallion' like all the rest of the fancy, white-coated officers about him, while they were already on their way to becoming 'front-swine'. His innocent young heart could have cried out loud at the injustice of it all. Instead he trailed miserably off to *Oberleutnant* Neurath's office to receive the first orders of his new job.

Christian Jungblut had known he was going to be a sailor from that morning on his fourth birthday when his father, 'the Captain', had presented him with a sailor suit, complete with the cap and its long black tails, bearing in gold the legend *Doerfflinger*. For even at that early age he had been aware that it had once been his father's ship, the ship in which he had fought that great battle which had cost him his right arm and brought his naval career to a sudden end.

For two whole years he had proudly worn that miniature naval uniform until he had been admitted into the *Volksschule* and had been forced, to the accompaniment of tears, to change into 'mufti', as his father had always called civilian clothes. But already the pattern had been set. By the time he was nine he was an expert swimmer, a good oarsman and was already sailing his own home-made sailing boat on the River Spree in his native Berlin.

But that was not all that Christian Jungblut was learning in those bitter years of the early thirties, with six million Germans unemployed and the Communists and Nazis fighting each other daily in the streets of strife-torn Berlin. 'A great injustice has been done to our beloved country, Christian,' his father would lecture him in the evenings when he came back, worn and grey, from the hated insurance offices, where the former *Kapitan zur See* was lucky enough to have found employment as a minor claims clerk. 'Not only have the Western Allies, Britain, France and America, ruined our economy, they have taken away our pride too.' He would shake his head sadly and look almost longingly at his old cruiser hanging on the wall of his study, still decorated with black crape from the day it had been sunk in that great battle. 'What are we now, but a mess of political thugs wearing different coloured shirts? Our army is limited to one hundred thousand men, the Allies do not allow us to have an air force or a submarine service, and the navy' – invariably his father would choke at the mention of his old service and his faded eyes would flood with tears – 'is a collection of antiquated ships built before 1914.'

Year in, year out, that lesson would be hammered home: the German Navy had been ruined and rendered impotent by the victorious Allies after World War One. And Christian Jungblut knew in his heart of hearts that he was predestined to be one of those who would one day rebuild that navy which his father loved so much.

In 1936, one year after his father had died, when his mother could no longer afford to keep him at the *gymnasium* on her meagre widow's pension, he had volunteered for the new *Kriegsmarine* now expanding rapidly under Hitler's rearmament plan. His mother had not objected, for she had already found a new lover and was preparing to move south with him to the Black Forest. Christian had felt no resentment. All his attention and emotions had been concentrated on his career in the Navy.

It had been hard, very hard. Their instructors on the Baltic island of Duenholm, where the training school for officer-cadets was located, were all failed officer-cadets themselves. Now as petty officers they took out their own failure on these would-be officers.

As every new day of torture began with the shrill of the bosun's whistle, they would be chased out of their bunks and into the showers, taunted and bullied by the petty officers: 'Come on you greenbeaks, what do you call that worm between yer legs . . ? When you piss, you know, it ain't a waterfall . . . Hurry up there, man, or I'll burn yer naked arse for you . . !' And so it would go on all the long day. Shrilling bosun's whistles, shouting, red-faced petty officers, everything done at the double, drill and more drill . . .

Even at night they had little rest. If the duty petty officer doing his rounds took it in his head to exercise his authority, he could have them doing knee-bends or push-ups at two o'clock in the morning or preparing for the 'gala ball', changing at top speed into one of their various uniforms picked at random by the sadistically grinning petty officer.

Then there was the 'Valley of Death' for an infringement of the rules such as not having the requisite number of studs in their boots or having failed to polish the metal buttons of their undershirts until they gleamed like mirrors: a five kilometre run up a hill, its slope a sea of clinging mud, weighed down with fifty pounds of equipment, rifle, steel helmet and gas-mask. Red-faced, streaming with sweat, breath coming in hectic gasps, they would stagger on as the petty officers hosed the slope to make it even slicker, knowing that if they fell out, they would be dismissed from the school and disgraced. Indeed there were rumours circulating through their ranks that more than one failed cadet had been unable to bear the shame of it all and had committed suicide.

'You see, Jungblut,' one of the few friendly and humane instructors called Ostmann, a big, slow East Frisian, had once explained to him when he had been close to despair at the cruelty and injustice of their training, 'in the Navy there are only two types: sharks and little fishes.' He had taken his clay pipe out of his mouth with a hand like a small steam-shovel and had pointed it almost accusingly at Christian. 'And do you know, Jungblut, what sharks do?'

'*Nein, Herr Obermaat*,' he had replied, his handsome young face puzzled under the cropped blond hair.

'They eat the little fishes up, Jungblut, that's what they do! For you, we are the sharks. But one day you'll be a shark, if you graduate, and then it will be your turn to eat up the little fishes. Remember that, Jungblut . . . Sharks and little fishes . . .' As the months and years had passed and he had graduated from school to school, those words of the big slow East Frisian had lingered in his brain: '*In the Navy there are only two types: sharks and little fishes*!'

Now it seemed to Ensign Christian Jungblut, as he waited outside *Oberleutnant zur See* Neurath's office for his orders, smarting with the injustice of his posting, that once again he, the 'little fish', had fallen into the hands of yet another shark. When would it ever end?

But unknown to an unhappy Christian, his fate was already being decided a hundred or more kilometres away off the coast of Denmark. Soon he would escape this particular elegant, arrogant shark now emerging from his office to announce superciliously, 'Well, Ensign Jungblut, here is your first duty. Till further notice, you will be responsible for ferrying senior officers back and forth to the quay and other ships in the launch. Apparently,' he added as a parting shot, 'no petty officer can be found to do the job. *Now move it*!'

Christian 'moved it', his heart almost broken . . .

CHAPTER 7

Oberleutnant von Arco spat over the side of the rusty conning-tower for luck yet once again, trying not to notice the awesome stink of decay coming up from the interior of the U-69. Now as the sky started to flush the first ugly white of a new dawn, to reveal the faint smudge of land on the horizon, the U-69 proceeded at a snail's pace through the minefield laid by the Tommies.

On both sides of the battered U-boat Hanssen had posted all free hands, either as look-outs or as 'pole-vaulters' as he had called them in a weakly humorous attempt to break the almost unbearable tension on board the ship. The 'pole-vaulters' were armed with boat-hooks. It was their task when a mine was spotted to edge the long pole between those deadly horns and gingerly push the ball of high explosive from the U-69's vulnerable hull. It was ticklish, nerve-racking work and already one of the younger ratings had broken and begun to sob like a child after ten long minutes of hard, tense labour trying to steer a mine away from the port side.

On the bridge von Arco swept the sea to their front with his binoculars, anxiously searching for any more of the damned things, knowing that safety was almost reached; but knowing too that here where the channel narrowed and the tidal race became fiercer they were entering the area of greatest danger. For here the mines could be upon them in the quickening sea before they had any chance to take counter-measures.

Suddenly there again was that dread sound: a rusty scraping along the hull.

'*Stop both*!' von Arco reacted immediately, feeling his nerves begin to jingle electrically. They had contacted another mine.

'Over here, sir,' Maydag sang out, pole at the ready, like a lancer preparing to spear some unfortunate infantryman.

Von Arco focused his glasses urgently, a cold trickle of sweat coursing down his spine. A dark bobbing object, spiked with horns, leapt into his view. Von Arco swallowed. If the damned thing caught up in the planes to the rear of it, that would be that.

Slowly, steadily, the boat continued to drift. Now the mine was only ten metres from the plane. Von Arco watched as if mesmerized, hardly daring to breathe, as the little torpedo-man braced himself and then millimetre by millimetre pushed the brass hook of his pole towards the ugly, dark metal globe. Von Arco swallowed hard. If he slipped and hit one of those deadly horns with the hook, it would all be over for them. Suddenly he found himself praying urgently for the first time since he had renounced religion as 'Jewish mumbo-jumbo' to join the Hitler Youth.

Down below Maydag controlled his breathing with difficulty, while next to him the giant Hamburger Frensen watched in tense silence. Now the mine was between two of the hooks. In one moment he would thrust against the surface of the mine itself, but if the mine moved . . . He didn't think that particular overwhelming thought to an end. Instead, he tensed his grip on the slippery pole with wet, sweating hands and, biting his bottom lip until the blood came, pushed forward. The mine bobbed up a little. He fought off the almost overwhelming impulse to close his eyes. Sweat trickled down his face. A vein began to tick frantically at his temple. His breath came in short, hectic gasps.

Suddenly there was the harsh grating of metal against metal. He let out a heartfelt sigh of relief, his legs like water. Next to him Frensen breathed out hard and grunted, 'Shit on the shingle! That took yer long enough, piss pansy!'

But Maydag hadn't the strength to answer. Instead he concentrated on the task of shoving the mine away beyond the protruding plane and into the U-69's wake.

Up on the bridge, von Arco wiped the sweat from his brow, face still drawn and ashen with tension. Once more he focused his glasses, knowing that the narrows were full of the damned deadly things. It was then that he saw the little craft. A fishing boat, probably Danish, chugging slowly through the sea, unaware that it was in mortal danger.

Suddenly von Arco's brain raced electrically. He saw the solution to their problem with the instant clarity of a vision. Of course, that was the way out! He did not hesitate. 'Bridge,' he barked to Hein, the engineer-officer, who was in charge below while Hanssen slept, 'full ahead!'

He could hear Hein's sharp intake of breath and for a moment nothing happened.

'Did you hear me, man? I said full ahead!'

'*Jawohl*, *Herr Oberleutnant*,' Hein cried, voice clearly revealing the fact that he was deadly scared and thought, too, that von Arco had gone mad with the strain.

But von Arco had not gone mad this icy dawn. Cost what it may, he was going to save the U-69 and his own skin.

Aghast, the men on the deck stared at von Arco as the diesels beat into action once more and the U-69 started to move ahead again. 'Christ on a crutch, Maydag!' Frensen exclaimed, shoving his cap to the back of his shaven skull, 'what's the matter with that fart? Hasn't he got all his cups in the cupboard?'

But von Arco had not gone crazy. Indeed, at that moment he was probably the sanest man on board the U-

69 and determined that the battered boat would carry him back to land and safety . . .

It took Hanssen a long time to realize that the U-69 was moving again, and faster than she should in a minefield. He was exhausted from the events of the last few days and sleep would not relinquish its grasp upon his worn-out body. Somehow he was still that fifteen-year-old cadet in his old-fashioned 'father murderer'*, watching with a mixture of schoolboyish glee and sadness at the trick they had played on the Tommies as their ship, its scuttles open, slowly started to sink beneath the waves at Scapa Flow. Close by in the rowing boat someone was saying over and over again, 'now the Tommies know that we of the Imperial Navy will never surrender!' And then he was being sea-sick for the first – and last – time in his life and a grey-bearded old *Maat* was chortling, 'Look at young Hanssen. He must be an animal-lover feeding the fish like that. Ha ha!'

Suddenly he sat bolt-upright and wide awake in the tight bunk divided from the rest of the U-boat by a simple green baize curtain. '*Himmel, Arsch und Wolkenbruch*!' he cursed, 'What is von Arco about?' Grabbing his battered white cap he swung himself out of the bunk and swayed his way through the sub to where a pale-faced Hein stood next to the periscope. 'Hein, why the devil are you moving at this speed? Why, you must be travelling at eight knots at least!'

'Orders from *Oberleutnant* von Arco, sir,' the fat little engineer answered and there was no mistaking the fear in his voice. He too knew the risk they were taking.

Angrily Commander Hanssen pushed by the engineer and started to clamber up the ladder into the new day. He

* Stiff wing collar as worn by the Imperial Navy

caught a glimpse of von Arco's harshly handsome face, set in a savage grin of anticipation and framed by the scared faces of the bridge watch. Then he was there on the bridge, following the direction of von Arco's gaze.

Directly ahead, perhaps some two or three hundred metres away, and heading straight for the coast and safety, there was a small fishing smack, the gulls wheeling and diving in her wake as the crew threw away the waste from the fish they were gutting. Obviously it was returning from a night fishing trip, its hold filled with herrings or sprats. A small harmless boat, crewed by a handful of middle-aged family men too old to have been called up for the forces, if they were German that is, for the smack carried no flag to identify its nationality.

'What's your game, von Arco?' Hanssen rasped, taking his gaze off the smack. 'Why in heaven's name are you travelling at this speed through a minefield?'

Von Arco turned to him, eyes full of cunning and triumph. 'But don't you see, sir?' he exclaimed, all too clearly very proud of himself. 'Why risk our own precious necks when we can get some other mug to do the dirty work for us?'

Hanssen looked at him in totally shocked disbelief. 'Do you mean to say,' he stuttered, his face crimson, 'that you are using that boat up there to clear the way for us?'

'Yes sir!' Von Arco's confident smile was still glued to his face. 'Her bow wave will clear any mine in both our paths. If it does not . . .' He shrugged easily and didn't complete his sentence.

For one long moment Hanssen didn't speak; he *couldn't*. Suddenly he was aware that von Arco had absolutely no concept of what was right and wrong. He lacked morality and he lacked a soul. Von Arco was a one hundred per cent product of the New Order – a National Socialist monster who would calmly and unthinkingly walk over dead bodies to achieve his aims. 'But you can't mean it, von Arco?' he stuttered finally, eyes full of disbelief.

'I certainly don't believe in Father Christmas, sir. What are the lives of a handful of middle-aged fishermen worth in comparison with those of forty highly-trained young men who will help to win the war for Germany? As our Führer often says, you can't make an omelette without breaking eggs.' He paused and looked at Hanssen's shocked face quite coolly, as if it was the most obvious thing on earth.

Hanssen recovered himself. '*Oberleutnant* von Arco, you are already under open arrest. I now order you from the bridge! I shall take charge of the ship. You will go below –'

The rest of his words were drowned by the roar as the little fishing smack hit a mine. Hanssen swung round. The bow of the smack seemed to leap out of the water in a ball of vicious red flame. With startling suddenness she began to sink. There was a horrid sucking noise, a wild boiling of the water and she was gone, huge obscene bubbles of trapped air exploding on the suddenly littered surface the only markers of her passing.

A moment later they were sailing through the pathetic flotsam of the sunken boat: bottles, pieces of netting, what looked like a leg of salt pork – and a dead man, bobbing up and down on the waves, false teeth bulging out of his mouth stupidly, eyes open and gazing sightlessly into a merciless dawn.

Thirty minutes later the U-69 was through and on the bridge Hanssen could see the white-painted patrol boats hurrying out to meet the submarine, obviously alerted by what had happened to the fishing boat. Glumly he lowered his glasses, feeling very, very old. They had made it. But somehow, although his own life had been at stake, he felt – no, he *knew* – that the price in innocent lives had been too high.

Below, von Arco had no such scruples. Squatting on his bunk, sipping his 'nigger sweat'*, he gazed at his tense, bearded face in the little square of mirror hung over the bed. 'This is the way it is going to be,' he whispered fervently at his own image. 'This is how Germany will win the war. Through ruthlessness and cunning.' He paused and then breathed those two magic words which sent the blood racing through his body with an almost unbearable electric excitement: '*Sieg Heil* . . !'

* Coffee

CHAPTER 8

'Looks as if they've got him, sir,' the old *Obermaat* said and sucked reflectively on his pipe, the brief-case chained to his wrist resting on his ample paunch. 'Poor shit!' He took the pipe out from between his blackened teeth and spat over the side, as the English bomber started to trail deep black smoke across the harbour.

Here and there the flak guns which surrounded Kiel still pounded away, flecking the grey sky with bursts of brown smoke, but for the most part they had fallen silent now. They knew the lone Wellington couldn't escape.

Jungblut nodded to the sailor at the controls of the launch and he decreased speed. Standing spread-legged at the bow, his cap-ribbons fluttering in the breeze, the second of the two ratings of Jungblut's command prepared to fend off the quay with his boat-hook.

It was twenty-four hours now since Christian Jungblut had taken over command of the launch and he was heartily sick of it. Back and forth across the harbour all day long, ferrying anything from condescending officers' wives going to lunch with their husbands to elderly paymasters going to see their doctors about their piles. Now he even had petty officers as passengers. Christian sighed heavily. This was not the kind of naval career he had visualized for himself when he had first donned that mini-uniform as a four-year-old. There was nothing dangerous or glamorous about being a jumped-up naval bus conductor!

The elderly *Obermaat* creaked to his feet and grinned,

obviously guessing what was going through the young Ensign's mind. 'Don't worry, sir. The first fifty years are the worst. Thanks for the lift.' Cautiously, as befitted an old man, he grasped the dripping iron railing and pulled himself up.

Above, the cadence of the Wellington's one remaining engine changed to a despairing whine. More smoke began to pour from it. It was going into its dive of death. 'Poor shit!' He echoed the *Obermaat's* words of pity. Enemy that the Tommy pilot was, he could feel for him at this moment as he fought desperately to raise the stricken plane before it plunged to its inevitable end.

'There it goes!' the old *Obermaat* cried, standing above him on the slick, wet quay and pointing a dirty finger to the sky.

The two-engined bomber seemed to be standing on its nose. With startling suddenness purple flame seared its length like a giant blow-torch. The port wing fell off like a metal leaf. Abruptly its gleaming perspex nose fell one hundred and eighty degrees and plunged straight for the water, a blazing metal coffin. With a tremendous thud it slammed into the earth on the opposite shore of the sound. The boat trembled violently. A moment later a thick black mushroom of smoke started to ascend to the grey sky. Above Jungblut, the old *Obermaat* raised his hand to his peaked cap in salute and then stumped off.

Christian Jungblut's frown deepened. Now he was depressed even more by what had just happened. At least that poor chap who had piloted the plane in its lone, daring attack on the German fleet spaced out in Kiel Harbour had died fighting. He, on the other hand, seemed fated to die of boredom. Suddenly he made up his mind, although it was against Neurath's orders. 'You, Leading Hand,' he called to the seaman at the controls, 'you're in charge for an hour.'

The Leading Hand, one of the older, sly sort, with a

cocky grin on his skinny mug and half a smoked cigarette tucked behind his ear, contrary to regulations, smiled knowingly. 'There's a nice discreet place just behind the *Hauptbahnhof, Herr Fähnrich,*' he suggested. 'Not expensive and reserved for officers, except if you happen to be handsome like yours truly,' he added cheekily, winking.

Christian's frown deepened even more. At this particular moment on this grey, depressingly wet day, cheap port whores were the last thing that interested him. He just wanted to get away for an hour from playing bus conductor to half the fleet. 'Check the launch, Leading Hand,' he snapped briskly, 'and have a look at that front fender. It's hanging loose.'

'*Jawohl, Herr Fähnrich,*' the Leading Hand snapped back jumping to attention, thumbs pressed tightly to the sides of his blue pants.

Christian Jungblut touched his hand to his cap in reply and added as a parting shot, 'And oh yes, take that disgusting lung torpedo from behind your right ear. It's against dress regulations.' And with that he was gone, leaving the Leading Hand, he knew instinctively, smouldering and making obscene gestures behind his back. He didn't care. For an hour at least, he was free of the shitting launch!

Oberleutnant zur See Neurath placed the folder in front of Doenitz and said respectfully, 'The *OKM** will announce the loss of the U-69 at sixteen hundred hours this afternoon, sir.'

Doenitz looked up, his hard face set. He had a son himself in the submarine service. Losses always affected him personally. But it was not only that. The loss of the U-

* Naval HQ

69 meant that he would have to start all over again, if his bold plan was going to succeed.

'Are we quite sure that the U-69 has been sunk? Commander Hanssen is a sly fox. He fought the Reds in the Spanish Civil War. It is not the first time he has been under fire, Neurath.'

'I know, sir. He is a very experienced captain. But there has been nothing heard from the U-69 for forty-eight hours. I think we can conclude that she has been sunk.'

Doenitz nodded. 'So be it.' He accepted the fact without any further comment. 'I want an immediate conference called of all senior U-boat captains currently in harbour for, say, eight hundred hours tomorrow morning. Time is running out on Project X. We must start all over again, but quickly.'

'Yessir, I shall attend to it immediately. Any further orders, sir?'

'Yes, Neurath. You'd better get me Commander Hanssen's home address. I shall write to his wife personally. We will have the letter delivered by officer-courier. It is better that way.'

'Yessir,' Neurath answered and went out swiftly to check the files for Hanssen's address; and it was thus occupied that he saw the carefree young officer, dressed in his first class uniform, complete with dirk, sauntering casually by the crowd of excited little Hitler Youths in their short pants, eagerly collecting the shrapnel that had fallen from the exploding anti-aircraft guns. Neurath frowned and checked his watch. His frown deepened. The young swine was not scheduled to be off duty yet. He swung round sharply to the petty officer (records) standing there attentively. 'Take over,' he commanded. 'Find Lieutenant-Commander Hanssen's address immediately. I have something else to attend to.'

'Yessir.'

Hurriedly Neurath reached for his elegant peaked cap,

pulled down his tunic and went out, face set and hard. The sentries at the gate clicked to attention. He acknowledged their salute and stepped out into the street, pushing aside the kids collecting souvenirs. Across the way firemen in steel helmets were pulling what was left of the Tommies from the wreck of the Wellington and piling the charred bodies on a horse-drawn cart as if they were logs of wood.

But First-Lieutenant Neurath had no eyes for the kids or the dead Tommies. His gaze was concentrated on the young officer staring at the dirty water of the harbour, hands dug into his pockets, whistling softly to himself as if he had not a care in the world. '*Fähnrich* Jungblut!' he snapped.

Christian Jungblut swung round as if he had been shot and snapped to attention when he saw who it was, his handsome face flushing. 'Sir!' he barked.

Neurath clicked his fingers angrily. 'Is that any way to report, Ensign?' he demanded. 'Report correctly as regulations prescribe!'

Jungblut swallowed hard. '*Fähnrich zur See Jungblut meldet sich zur Stelle*!' he cried using the traditional formula when addressing a senior officer. He stopped and waited expectantly.

Neurath let him wait, savouring his power over the flushed young man as he stood there standing rigidly to attention like a young recruit.

Now the driver of the cart bearing the charred bodies of the RAF crew was flicking his whip and urging his tired old nag forward and the Hitler Youth boys had stopped their souvenir-hunting to stare at the dead Englishmen.

'Ensign Jungblut,' Neurath said at last, 'have you any explanation for having abandoned your post? You were supposed to remain on duty for another hour yet. Please answer.'

Christian Jungblut swallowed hard again. 'There were

no more passengers scheduled, sir. So I thought I'd take a little stroll.'

'You *thought* Ensign!' Neurath said angrily, face flushing. 'You are not paid to *think*! You are paid to *carry out orders* – to the letter! Don't you realize, Ensign, that you have committed an offence?'

'Yessir,' Christian answered miserably.

'How can one trust a person like you, Jungblut, I ask myself. How can one honestly post you to a fighting ship when you cannot carry out the simplest order correctly? Don't you understand that it is vital that an officer must be one hundred and ten per cent correct? He must be more papal than the pope!' Neurath hammered home his point relentlessly and at that moment Christian would not have cared if the earth had opened up and had swallowed him for ever. Neurath was 'making a sow' of him in public, in front of the grinning kids who now found him more interesting than the dead Tommies. God in heaven, how humiliating! Would the damned rear-echelon stallion never finish? 'You will have to be punished,' Neurath was saying. 'There is no doubt about that. You have committed a serious offence and –' Suddenly his harsh words trailed away to nothing.

Up the sound there came the shrill cry of a klaxon, followed an instant later by the deep bass hooting of a ship's siren. Now more and more of the craft anchored in the sound were taking up the welcome. Everywhere there was the noise of ship's whistles, sirens and klaxons. Even the bells in the little church across the way had begun to toll joyously.

Neurath's mouth fell open as he spotted the object of this sudden, jubilant reception. Out of the corner of his eyes, while still standing rigidly to attention, Christian followed the direction of his astonished gaze.

A battered submarine, listing heavily, its superstructure shattered and trailing, the red paint undercoat showing in streaks through the splintered grey surface paint, the pennants of victory fluttering in the breeze, was sailing its way slowly through the crowded sound. Strain as he could Christian could not make out its number; for the conning-tower, pocked with shrapnel marks, was covered with rust and the light green shine of algae, as if the submarine had been underwater for months.

Leutnant zur See Neurath provided that number for him, however. In a low, incredulous voice he gasped, his arrogant face shocked and ashen, '*Mein Gott* . . . it's Hanssen!'

Christian's heart skipped a beat. He was saved.

'*Hanssen and the U-69*,' Neurath choked, Ensign Jungblut forgotten. '*Hanssen and the U-69 . . . they've come back*!' Next moment he was actually running full-tilt back to the barracks to report the news to Doenitz, leaving a suddenly deflated Christian Jungblut to stare at the battered boat as if he were watching an apparition. Slowly, almost painfully, the U-69 limped to her berth, the crew lining her deck staring into space, apparently unaware of the noise and the cheering on all sides.

Ensign Jungblut pulled himself together. He clicked to attention once more. Proudly he raised his hand to his cap to salute his new ship, the U-69 . . .

BOOK TWO

A Mission is Proposed

'The Orkneys are the arsehole of the world – and Scapa is stuffed right up it!'

Wartime British sailor's view of Scapa Flow

CHAPTER 1

'*Ensign Jungblut, sir*!' Christian snapped and saluted the tough-looking Captain whose face revealed a strange sickly-white patch where he had shaved off his beard, prior to meeting Doenitz.

Hanssen regarded him with those witty blue eyes of his and, apparently liking what he saw, said, 'Good to have you aboard, Jungblut.' He reached out and Jungblut found himself taking a hand that was hard, firm and dry. Instinctively he knew he was going to like the stocky little Skipper. He definitely wasn't one of the sharks. 'I'm going ashore now, Jungblut. So I'll leave you to *Oberleutnant* von Arco.' Suddenly he frowned as if he had thought of something unpleasant. 'He'll give you your instructions.' With that he was gone, climbing over the side to where Maydag and Frensen waited in the bobbing rubber dinghy.

Jungblut hesitated only a moment before clambering into the submarine's interior, his nostrils assailed for the first time by that terrible stench of decay, sweat and oil which he would come to know so well. A tall, arrogant officer was standing there waiting for him dressed in a grey leather jacket and wrinkled trousers, his boots almost bleached white by the salt water.

Again Jungblut reported and waited.

Von Arco took his time, running his gaze from Christian's face down the length of his uniform, complete with ensign's dirk, to his highly polished shoes. Then he spoke. 'Take off that rubbish for a start. We're not going to a fancy dress ball, you know, Jungblut. Right, now let this be understood from the beginning. You are a nobody here and virtually good for nothing. The most junior rating on the boat knows more than you do, Jungblut. You are simply supercargo and a useless waste of valuable air. Clear?'

Jungblut swallowed hard and managed to say, '*Klar, Herr Oberleutnant.*' Again he was one of the little fishes fallen into the grasp of a shark.

'Your task on board is to get used to things and pick up our ways swiftly. Soon we will be sailing once more and if I find your face doesn't fit, Jungblut, then you stay behind. Is that understood?'

'*Jawohl, Herr Oberleutnant.*'

'All right, find yourself some overalls. One of the petty officers will show you around. Dismiss!'

Up above as he balanced on deck, Commander Hanssen frowned. Typical von Arco, he told himself as the tirade ended and the new recruit disappeared, presumably in the direction of the stores. Even though von Arco was in disgrace himself he could not resist making life miserable for Jungblut. But soon things would change, he consoled himself. He wanted von Arco off the U-69. By now Doenitz would have read his initial report and would be prepared to take appropriate steps against von Arco. 'All right,' he commanded as he stepped onto the swaying little craft, 'off we go. When we arrive I'll give you two rogues one hour of shore-leave and then I expect you back to row me to the boat. Get it?'

'Got it!' the two of them roared in unison and bent over their paddles, big grins of anticipation on their pale, shaven faces. Hanssen returned their grin. He knew where their first port of call would be. What was it the old salts said about the leaveman going home to his missus? The *second* thing the leaveman does is to take off his pack.

They'd be in the nearest brothel in zero-comma-nothing seconds!

The guided tour of the U-69 was a sobering experience for Christian Jungblut. His initial enthusiasm for his new ship soon vanished as he began to realize just exactly what he had let himself in for.

In a few moments he had lost his bearings altogether. He banged his head against pipes and ducts, handcranks, wheels and a myriad other instruments as he crept through the bulkheads trying to understand what each pipe was meant for and where it led.

'There are three Lords* to each bunk, Ensign,' the petty officer explained, a big grin on his tough face at the newcomer's obvious confusion. 'In the case of the stokers it's two men to one bunk. As soon as one turns out on watch, his mate creeps into the bunk. Might provide yer with a few little itchy bees but it ain't half warm.'

'Yes, yes, thanks for the information, *Obermaat*,' Christian answered, trying to absorb this whole new range of slang with its 'Lords' for sailors, 'bees' for lice and so on.

'The stores we stow everywhere, Ensign,' the petty officer continued, indicating the spaces between the torpedo tubes.

'Even in there. But we've got to be right careful. We've got to stow the gear according to a fixed plan so that the boat is kept trimmed when we dive. And we've got to make sure that they don't shift, otherwise we go straight down.' He grinned at Jungblut. 'And then we don't come up again!'

In a moment Christian realized what he had let himself in for. Not only were they fighting the enemy in the U-boat service, but they were also fighting nature itself. No

* Sailors

wonder the Lords called their craft, with grim humour, 'tin coffins'. For that was exactly what they could well turn out to be. Slowly the two men worked their way through the submarine's four compartments, Christian growing more confused by the moment, until finally they arrived back at the fourth and smallest one: the conning-tower containing the attack periscope torpedo computer and helm.

There *Oberleutnant* von Arco was waiting for him. 'All right, Jungblut,' he barked. 'You have seen the U-69. Now let us start your training. You see that pipe over there?' He indicated a pipe close to the floor which had been lagged as if it might have been punctured at some time or other.

'Yessir. I see it,' Jungblut answered promptly. Next to him the *Obermaat* started to grin. He knew what was coming. The new Ensign was going to be initiated like they all were - the hard way.

'Right then. This is your first task. You must trace the course of that pipe and find out where it comes from. When you have done that, make a thorough check of it and if it needs cleaning, do so.'

'Yessir,' Jungblut answered, wondering where he would start and why the grinning petty officer was now holding his nose as if there was a terrible smell coming from somewhere. 'Do you think I'll have to go under the plates, sir?'

'You can go to the bottom of the damned sound as far as I am concerned, Ensign!' von Arco snapped angrily. 'Now get on with it!'

Five minutes later a hapless Christian Jungblut found himself kneedeep in stale urine and turds. The pipe led straight to the bilges into which the crew emptied their slops when enemy action prevented them using the 'heads'!* Ruefully he told himself his career with the fighting U-69 had not started off very auspiciously.

* Latrines

*

Neither had Commander Hanssen's interview with Commodore Karl Doenitz. Of course the 'Big Lion' had received him warmly – or as warmly as that cold-natured man with ice instead of blood in his veins ever could. He had risen shaken the U-boat Skipper's hand with one that was cold as the grave, expressed the usual sentiments, offered him a *doornkaat*, toasting him in the chilled pale liquid, and then said, without any further preliminaries, 'I will take no steps against Oberleutnant von Arco, Hanssen, do you understand that?'

Hanssen realized he must have shown his surprise, for Doenitz barked, his thin cruel lips moving as if by a tightly oiled spring, 'You heard me correctly, Hanssen. There will be no court-martial!'

'But sir,' Hanssen protested. 'The man shot at unarmed seamen in the water.'

'He showed the new ruthlessness,' Doenitz corrected him coldly, 'that will win us this war. We Germans are far too soft. What do we say? "The German has a heavy hand and a soft heart. The Englishman has a soft hand but a very, very hard heart." To win the sea war we must break that Englishman's heart and the only way we can do it is to be as ruthless as the Tommies have always been and still are. Is that absolutely clear?'

'Certainly sir but –'

'No *buts*!' Doenitz interrupted him harshly, already making up his mind that good officer that he might be, Commander Hanssen was not the man to carry out the great plan. Someone else would have to carry out the mission in his place. At that moment Hanssen's fate was sealed. He would die an obscure death – for nothing. 'Now then, Hanssen, let us forget *Oberleutnant* von Arco and discuss the mission. What do you suggest is the best plan of attack . . ?'

*

Von Arco sprang up the steps of the big old house two at a time. Now the U-69 was forgotten. All that he could think about was her pale naked body and those wonderful ample breasts. He shot a look to left and right. The dark landing was empty. His thumb shot out and he pressed the bell. '*Frau Oberleutnant Neurath.*'

The wife of Doenitz's Adjutant opened the door immediately. She was dressed in her coat and was wearing a hat as if she were just preparing to go out. She gasped when she saw him and said 'you', her hand flying to her mouth as if she were surprised or shocked. 'Egon, you . . . I thought you were –'

'Dead!' He completed the sentence for her, taking in those wonderful breasts of hers and feeling his heart beginning to beat frantically with excitement. Of course, he had had other women since he had taken up with her but she still excited him the most. He supposed it was because of the risk and the knowledge that he was cuckolding that arrogant rear-echelon stallion Neurath. 'You know what they say, Eva,' he said, pushing by her into the big apartment, 'weeds don't die easily.'

'But I was just about to go –'

He smothered her protest with a kiss, his hands feeling automatically for her breasts as he kicked the door closed with the heel of his right shoe.

'But if Kurt were to come,' she gasped, her nipples already growing hard under his fingers, her breath coming in short, hectic gasps.

'He won't,' von Arco assured her, his voice thick with lust. 'He's busy with my Skipper and the rest of the U-boat skippers. There's a big flap on. Come on. It's been a long time. Into the bedroom!' He half-propelled her into the big bedroom, very feminine with its frills and lace curtains and very seductive. 'Hurry up. Get your clothes off, Eva.' He started to fumble with his flies.

'My God, Egon,' she sobbed, half excited, half fearful. 'You can't expect a woman –'

He stifled her protest with a savage kiss and pushed her backwards onto the bed. For one moment he grinned at her husband's photo on the bedside table and then he was ripping feverishly at her clothes . . .

One kilometre away Frensen and Maydag emerged from the brothel whistling happily, Frensen mopping his sweat-lathered brow with a pair of red silk knickers that he had stolen from the whore whom he had just 'pleasured' as he put it. 'By the Great Whore of Buxtehude,' he proclaimed to no one in particular, 'where the dogs whistle through their arses – *that was good*! God, I had so much ink in my pen' – he grabbed his bulging crotch significantly – 'that I didn't know who to write to first!'

'Mine could have swallowed a trombone – *sideways*!' Maydag said with modest pride, gaze fixed demurely on the pavement. 'I think she fell in love with me right off.'

Frensen looked down at his shipmate scornfully. 'Fell in love with yer shitting wallet more likely!' he sniffed. 'Anyway that's that.' He dabbed his brow with the knickers once more. 'Bit of skat* tonight with those greenbeaks at the naval barracks and I'll have enough money for another bit of the pearly gate later on.' He sucked his teeth thoughtfully. 'Might get meself a couple of whores at once tonight.'

'Mine sez I can have it for nothing,' Maydag announced. 'I told yer she loved me.'

'Don't bother me with . . .' Frensen stopped suddenly. At the corner, the bigger of two steel-helmeted petty officers, both carrying carbines, was crooking his finger at

* A German card game

the two shipmates. 'Christ on a crutch!' he groaned. 'That's all we need - frigging chain-dogs! In God's name, Maydag, don't breathe on them with the load of schnaps you've just taken on board. Come on, let's face the music.'

Miserably the two comrades started to trail across the road to the hard-faced naval policemen. There would be no whores for them this night, or for a few nights to come.

Time was running out fast again for the U-69.

CHAPTER 2

'Stand at *ease!*' *Oberleutnant* Neurath barked. The men lining the deck of the U-69 slumped into the at ease position and waited. Standing a little apart from the rest, stinking to high-heaven, wretched and soaked in urine, Christian Jungblut took in a deep, grateful gulp of fresh sea air. Whatever the reason for this hurried summoning of the crew, it certainly saved him from any further work in those stinking, evil bilges.

Neurath mustered them with his keen gaze for an instant and then snapped, 'There's a flap on. No use denying it. Lt. Commander Hanssen is to remain ashore for a high level conference. For the time being *Oberleutnant* von Arco – wherever he might be at this moment – is to take over command.'

There was a muffled groan from the crew, for von Arco was universally detested. Frensen whispered to Maydag, 'Now the clock is really in the pisspot. Buy combs, Maydag, cos there's lousy times ahead.'

Solemnly Maydag nodded his head in agreement.

'As soon as *Oberleutnant* von Arco is found you will sail.'

There was another groan, for most of the crew had still to set foot on shore.

Neurath ignored the groans. What did the feelings and needs of these randy front-swine concern him? As long as they did their job efficiently nothing else mattered, he told himself. 'You will proceed to Hamburg for an instant refit. There will be no home leave on Commodore Doenitz' express order. Free hands, however, will be allowed local leave between dawn and dusk. I should imagine,' he added with a sneer, 'that should be time enough for you to bed down some filthy whore.'

'They build them big in the U-boat service,' Frensen ventured. 'We need more time than that to dance the mattress polka. We leave the quickies to the rear-echelon stallions.'

Christian grinned as Neurath flushed angrily. 'Who said that?' he cried.

Frensen's sole response was a contemptuously loud fart.

Neurath's arrogant face flushed an even deeper red. 'If I find the man who did that I shall –' But the rest of his threat was drowned by the squeal of car tyres. Next moment a taxi shuddered to a stop on the wet quay and von Arco came blundering out, thrusting money into the cabbie's hand while trying at the same time to button up his tunic. Neurath waited like a man sorely tried.

Casually, almost contemptuously, von Arco saluted Neurath. How could one respect a man, he told himself, who let his wife be bedded by another? '*Oberleutnant von Arco zur Stelle,*' he announced and then more casually, 'Where's the fire, Neurath?'

'A flap at HQ,' Neurath answered, feeling at a disadvantage at the sight of the submariner's badge and the new ribbon of the Iron Cross, Second Class on von Arco's tunic while his was bare of any decoration. 'It's to do with the Scapa Flow project. You are to take charge of the U-69 while Commander Hanssen works with the planning group.'

Von Arco beamed. So Hanssen had not been able to pin a court-martial charge on him after all. And now he was to command the U-69. 'My orders?' he barked happily.

'You are to take her to Hamburg. The Howardt Works are already alerted. You have to ensure the refit is completed within the week.' Neurath lowered his voice.

'Things are moving on the other side of the North Sea. Doenitz is scared that the Tommies might get wind of what he intends. The op is to go ahead at top speed. Hence the hasty refit.'

Von Arco nodded sagely. 'All right then. I see your police have mustered the crew.' He flashed a quick glance at his watch. 'We sail within the hour.'

Neurath and he clicked to attention and exchanged formal salutes. But von Arco could not resist a parting thrust. As Neurath clattered down the gangway towards the waiting staff car von Arco called, 'Oh and by the way, *Herr Oberleutnant*, do give my regards to your charming lady wife when you see her next.'

'Yes, of course,' Neurath replied a little puzzled. When had von Arco, that arrogant swine with his head full of National Socialist nonsense, ever been interested in the social niceties?

Von Arco grinned and dismissed the fool. 'All right, Hein, don't just stand there. There's work to be done. Dismiss the crew and let's get on with it. Now move!'

The little engineer-officer moved, and as they dispersed to their duty stations Frensen groaned and mimicked a sinking ship by going down slowly to his knees, saying contemptuously, '*Don't panic* . . . sink the *Titanic*. Now the wet fart has really hit the side of the thunderbox . . .'

It certainly had. Right from the very start von Arco made it quite clear who was the master aboard the battered submarine. 'A new wind is blowing,' he announced once they had cleared the sound. 'For the time that I am in charge we will do it my way. And *my way* is one hundred per cent efficiency. All duties will be carried out at the double and woe betide any one of you, rating or petty officer, who fails me: I shall come down on the individual mercilessly. Be quite clear about that!'

Although all the men except Jungblut were trained and war-experienced, now he treated them as if they were still raw recruits. He kept the alarm bells jingling all the time as they limped down the coast of Schleswig-Holstein towards Hamburg. Even those in the 'heads' were not exempt. They had to jump to like the rest, cursing and pulling up their pants as they raced for their duty stations.

Von Arco tested their diving time. 'Five seconds to clear the bridge,' he would bark and the men would come flying down from above, one and one fifth seconds per man before the next one came tumbling to the deck.

'Flood!' he'd cry, stop-watch in hand. 'Come on Hein – flood!'

Eyes bulging from his head with the strain, face wet with sweat, Hein would watch the section indicators, willing them to light up and show 'ready to dive' on each dial.

Like cats the ratings would jump to the valve levers, twisting them open, crying out their – to Jungblut – incomprehensible lingo – 'five, four, three, two, one – both!' – while von Arco tensed over his watch until finally they would be going down and Hein would collapse against the bulkhead exhausted by all the play-acting.

But at dawn on the second day of their slow progress to Hamburg the play-acting stopped. Suddenly reality broke in and Christian Jungblut had his first taste of that violent action that he had been waiting for so expectantly for so long.

He was on the bridge when it happened. The morning was cold and grey with a light fog billowing across the sluggish green sea, land a faint smudge to their port. Stamping his feet to bring some life back to them, he was thinking longingly of a cup of steaming hot 'nigger sweat' when abruptly the hand to his right sang out, 'Flying boat to the port bow . . . She's diving fast . . !'

Instantly all of them flung up their glasses. Hein, in

charge, yelled, 'Sunderland . . ! *It's a Tommy Sunderland* . . ! *And she's spotted us*!'

'*Alaaarm* . . . *alaarm*!' someone screamed frantically. The klaxons started to shrill. Instantly all was controlled but hectic activity. One by one the bridge crew hurtled towards the deck below, sliding down the rails, their hands burning with the friction.

The hatch clanged shut. Water showered down on von Arco as Hein tumbled to the deck, the last of the bridge crew.

'Twenty-five fathoms . . . diving fast, sir! Thirty degree load!' the crewman sang out, eyeing his controls almost greedily.

Von Arco frowned. 'We've got to be down at least to fifty –'

The rest of his words were drowned by a hollow, rolling boom. The U-boat rocked violently. Christian, caught off guard, was sent flying and slammed painfully into the bulkhead.

'Take care, Ensign!' von Arco roared as if Christian's mishap had angered him.

'Sorry, sir,' he replied, wiping the sudden blood from his forehead and realizing as he staggered to his feet that something had gone wrong.

'Outboard air induction valve jammed,' the sudden, urgent cry confirmed. 'It doesn't close!'

Now the U-69 was sinking fast at an angle of thirty-odd degrees.

A scared machinist poked his head round the bulkhead, face glazed with sweat as if it had been greased. 'Sir we can't stop the leak!' he yelled, 'The head valve must be jammed!'

Von Arco reacted automatically. 'Blow all tanks!'

The crew gasped. Von Arco was going to bring her up and risk the Tommy's bombs!

'Both planes up! Surface!'

Jungblut tensed, feeling totally out of place and hardly

understanding the technical details of what was going on around him. He had never anticipated that action at the front would be like this. In his youthful imagination he had expected he would be fighting the Tommies with a gun in his hands; not fighting for his life underneath the sea with the enemy above them, unknown and unseen.

The U-69 failed to respond. Suddenly she started to tilt to stern alarmingly. Jungblut supported himself the best he could as stores and personal belongings cascaded down the central aisle. The nearest hydroplane operator was flung from his seat. Another followed, screaming obscenely. The U-69 was heading straight for the bottom of the Baltic!

'Stop blowing!' a wide-eyed, suddenly frightened von Arco yelled desperately. '*The boat is out of control!*'

The U-69 hit the bottom with a sudden thud. Instantly tons of water rushed through the leak with a terrifying roar. Jungblut gasped with shock. The lights flickered and went out leaving them in inky frightening darkness. Someone started to say a 'Hail Mary'.

For one long eternity they remained thus in a loud-echoing silence, broken only by the sound of the man praying in a thick Bavarian accent. Then a hollow voice drifted in from the stern as the lights went on again and Christian saw the ashen-faced men already clinging on to any available support like shipwrecked sailors, the deck around their feet awash with water and littered with food cans: 'Inboard air induction valve closed and secured, sir!'

Von Arco forced himself to be calm. 'Thank you,' he said. 'All men to the bow room,' he commanded.

Like mountaineers, the men started to labour up the steep slope of the boat, already beginning to cough and splutter as the poison fumes began to escape from the ruptured batteries. Thoroughly scared now, and feeling the grip on his chest, Christian started after the others.

A dead man lay in the next compartment with the crew making a little circle around him. He lay floating on his back, eyes closed and with not a mark on his body so that he might well have been sleeping gently. Christian stared down at the first dead man he had ever seen and felt that iron grip constricting his chest tighten even more. The man had been gassed.

Now the dirty, sweat-lathered crewmen secured themselves in the bows, hanging on to stanchions and whatever else they could find. Christian hanging on there with them noted that their pale faces showed no emotion now save, perhaps, anger. Now they waited, playing no role whatsoever save that of ballast while below, glimpsed as if from the top of a lift shaft, von Arco conferred with Hein in the control room on what to do next.

Five minutes later the two of them had made their decision. 'We have about enough oxygen to last four or five hours,' von Arco called up to them. 'I am going to divide the crew into two halves. You'll work in hourly shifts to bale out the water. If we can do that successfully and get the boat on an even trim then I am sure we can raise her. All right, Chief Petty Officer, divide the crew!'

Christian vomited miserably, his shoulders heaving with the effort. His head ached, he was black up to the elbows in diesel oil, and he was exhausted. Now he felt ashamed of himself as he retched in front of the eyes of the rest of his shift. Next to him the big muscular torpedo mate Frensen seemed to read his mind, for he patted Christian kindly on the shoulder and said in his deep waterfront bass, 'Don't worry about it, Ensign. Puke the muck up. This place is a frigging open sewer as it is!'

They had emptied three hundred and forty containers full of the black goo that flooded the boat, balancing the best they could on the slope, occasionally losing their grip and sliding helplessly across the plates. All the time they had gasped and choked like ancient asthmatics, the air steadily becoming thicker, stinking of oil, chlorine and urine. Now the first shift crouched there absolutely exhausted, half suffocated and half drowned, and still they hadn't righted the boat.

A cook passed among them, handing out cans. They refused the food. They were too exhausted to eat it. But they seized the cans of fruit greedily, draining them of their thick syrup and gasping with pleasure as it soothed their parched, choked throats.

'All right!' Von Arco's harsh voice cut into their weary reveries. 'Up top. Come on now. *Los* . . . anything to help the trim!'

Infinitely slowly, every fresh move made only by an effort of naked willpower, they began to ascend the boat, gasping for breath, pain-racked bodies lathered in sweat, fighting for holds on the oil-slick surface.

Once Christian slipped. His hand shot out and he screamed with the agony of it as his nails were ripped away. He hung there, sobbing with pain, eyes blinded with scalding tears. How much more of this terrible misery! Down below, the second shift laboured on, sobbing for breath, crying out angrily, while the Chief Petty Officer counted out the cans they had emptied: 'Twenty . . . twenty-one . . . twenty-two . . .' It seemed hopeless. Would they ever free the U-69?

Frensen was a tower of strength. More than once he grabbed an exhausted man just in time, preventing his slithering all the way down again. For a while he slung a rating who had been overcome by the deadly chlorine gas over his shoulder as if he were a child and clambered upwards with him. He even found the strength to regale them with his ribald experiences in the 'knocking shops of half the world', as he boasted proudly. Miserably the rest toiled onwards.

'Did I ever tell yer about the gash I had with two sets of tits?' Fensen was saying when it happened. The impossible occurred. There was a sudden flurry of bubbles. They exploded loudly in the forward tank. The whole boat shuddered. The climbers paused, wonder written all over their black, exhausted faces. *What was happening?*

Slowly, awesomely slowly, the U-69 started to move. That terrible slope gentled out. Now they were no longer hanging on grimly. The deck sank beneath their feet. The nightmarish climb was over. They straightened themselves up, new hope dawning in their reddened, lack-lustre eyes. Abruptly with a muted thud the bow descended and hit the bottom of the Baltic.

Christian sat down suddenly in the water. They had done it. They had the trim once again. Next to him Frensen gulped and said, 'Maybe there's a frigging God after all, mates.'

Maydag, who hadn't been within a kilometre of a church since the day as a ten-year-old he had been kicked out of Sunday school for trying to look up the teacher's skirts, nodded solemnly and said, 'Amen to that mate . . .'

CHAPTER 3

The compressed air hissed with a sound like an express train rushing through a station at full speed. Desperately Hein, the little engineer, let more and more escape as the gasping, choking men waited anxiously. Next to the engineer, von Arco clenched his fists painfully, feeling his heart racing madly. For God's sake let him raise the boat!

Nothing happened! The U-69 remained firmly glued to the bottom, some 150 metres beneath the surface of the Baltic. Someone groaned and a sweating, haggard rating next to Christian gasped, 'Can't stand much frigging more of this, Ensign!' He coughed thickly into his hand and expelled a mess of black, nauseating mucus. Hastily Christian turned his head away.

Slowly the stream of compressed air began to grow weaker. The hiss gave way to a soft whisper and finally it died away altogether. They had exhausted their supply of compressed air. For one long moment there was nothing but a heavy, brooding silence inside the trapped boat. Even Frensen was too discouraged to crack one of his obscene jokes. Von Arco looked at the engineer, blood trickling from where his nails had bitten into his palms.

Hein swallowed hard. 'All right,' he commanded, 'we're not giving up. This is what we are going to do. All the men to the bow. *Los . . . dalli . . . dalli*!'

The crew tumbled immediately to what he was attempting to do. In spite of their exhaustion and the lack of oxygen, they fought and pushed their way to the bow, stumbling through the littered ankle-deep water. Once there, Hein ordered them to double back to the aft. Hein wanted to turn the U-69 into a giant see-saw in the hope that in this way it would work itself free from the gluelike embrace of the bottom. Now stumbling, shoving, panting, gasping, coughing, sweat dripping down from their faces, the crew moved back and forth like stampeding steers from a western film, over and over again.

The boat stirred gently for the first time. Frensen raised a cheer. 'After me,' he yelled, 'the torpedo-mate's got a hole in his arse!'

The almost exhausted men cheered with him and stumbled after the big petty officer yet once again. Suddenly it happened. As they bolted into the bow torpedo room the stern began to lift. *The U-69 was working itself free*!

Gasping harshly for breath, their skinny, sweat-lathered bodies trembling all over as if they were suffering from some tropical fever, the crew staggered back to their duty stations while von Arco, biting his bottom lip, waited anxiously at the periscope. Next to him the engineer gazed hypnotically at the needle of the repaired depth gauge calling out the depths in a broken voice: '*Eighty metres . . . sixty-five metres . . . forty metres . . . Ten metres . . . Tower is free. Boat has surfaced . . .*' He leaned back against the bulkhead suddenly as if he was going to fall in a dead faint. He had done it!

A moment later von Arco had opened the hatch and precious, damp sea air, more wonderful than a draught of the most expensive French champagne, was streaming into the littered interior of the U-69.

'The good old Michaelis Church, Maydag,' Frensen said happily as he spotted the green, pointed steeple of the Hamburg church towering above the port city's skyline.

'One kilometre from there and you're in the *Reeperbahn.** By God and all His triangles, we're gonna play the two-backed beast tonight, old house. That we are.' He grabbed the front of his shabby old trousers to make his point quite clear, a big grin on his broad, humorous face as he gazed at his native city.

Maydag was not so sure about that 'two-backed beast'. 'It depends on the Skipper,' he objected. 'You know what he's like, the shit!' He spat gloomily over the side.

Frensen thrust up a middle finger like a hairy pork sausage and growled threateningly. 'You know what he can do? He can stick that up his narrow, aristocratic arse!'

But on this particular day *Oberleutnant* von Arco was going to cause no problems. As he squatted in the 'heads' once again he realized his upset stomach was caused by the frightening events of the previous day. His nerve was going and he knew it. He couldn't take much more of the U-boat Service. Inside his head a harsh little voice corrected him: 'You must hold on, Kuno. You must! Get the piece of tin and cure your throatache, then you can retire gracefully to some shore job and safety. But you must do the next mission and survive. *You must*!' Wearily von Arco, as he squatted there, his wretched bowels bubbling and groaning eerily, nodded his agreement. In the victorious post-war Germany an officer who hadn't 'cured his throatache' by winning the coveted Knight's Cross of the Iron Cross would never reach the highest ranks in the Navy or the Party, he knew that. If he was to make a successful career for himself he would have to overcome his fear and complete that mission which he knew would win for him the medal. One more mission and then he would say goodbye to Doenitz' U-boats. A few moments later he began to pump out his own waste with a hand that trembled violently. *Oberleutnant* von Arco's nerves had

* The city's red light district

about reached breaking point.

Surprisingly enough, as he washed himself prior to going ashore at the *Landungsbrucke* to carry out von Arco's orders, Ensign Christian Jungblut found that the frightening, violent experiences of the last forty-eight hours had left no trace on his psyche. As he looked at himself in the sliver of a mirror, noting that his 'submariner's beard' was coming on quite nicely, he told himself that he had weathered his first taste of combat well. His eyes were clear and his face possessed none of the haggard lines he could see on those of the rest of the crew. Perhaps, he told himself as he ran a wet comb through his blond hair, he had the makings of a good U-boat man in him after all.

'Well, Ensign,' the fat engineer Hein grinned at him as he ascended to the bridge, 'as soon as you can get to the stores buy yourself the submariner's badge. You're entitled to it now.'

Christian flushed with pride. He had gained the precious combat badge with less than seventy-two hours' combat experience. 'Do you think the Captain will agree to it, sir?' he asked.

Hein looked solemn. 'Which captain do you mean? Von Arco or Commander Hanssen?' he asked.

'*Oberleutnant* von Arco sir.'

'*He'll* agree, never fear,' Hein announced, remembering how terrified von Arco had looked as the U-69 had sunk to the bottom of the Baltic. 'Besides, you've been under fire and have experienced a rescue operation. You've earned it.'

'Thank you again, sir.'

'Don't mention it, Jungblut,' Hein said with an airy wave of his pudgy hand. 'Now remember your orders. Then get yourself a good meal – and a woman too, if you're lucky.' He winked knowingly. 'Report back to duty this evening. That's all.'

Eagerly Christian saluted and then he was off, smartly

marching across the battered deck to spring neatly onto the quayside. Behind him Hein smiled. Ensign Jungblut was going to be all right . . .

'What did you do before the war, Hein?' von Arco asked as they stood there on the bridge, smoking the last cigars of the day and listening to the muted noises of the great city, its black-out broken now and again by the dim blue lights of the trams or the sudden opening of some house door.

'I had just finished university. I was going to be a marine engineer with hopes of having a nice cushy number on the *Bremen* or one of the other luxury liners. You know,' he grinned in the darkness at the memory, 'where you do nothing but eat eight course dinners and bed rich American ladies.' He shrugged. 'But as I had done my military service in the U-boat arm that was the end of that.'

Von Arco puffed at his thin black cigar for a moment. From the quayside came the drunken singing of some lost sailor, full of pathetic, maudlin references to his 'Homeland' and the mother he would see no more. Von Arco's face contorted contemptuously. What a sentimental people the Germans were! Thank God the Führer was finally beginning to toughen and harden them. What was his new motto? 'As hard as Krupp steel, as tough as leather and as fleet as a greyhound'.

'Do you know what I was, Hein?' he asked suddenly.

'No sir.'

'The last piece of shit - the scum of the earth,' he said bitterly. 'First a cadet on a sailing ship. Hell with sails we called it. Scrubbing the decks with a toothbrush at ten below zero. If you were lucky, two hours sleep a day. Eating trash only fit for pigs. All that so I could qualify for the *Kriegsmarine* when there was one berth for every ten applicants. And why did I want to qualify, Hein?'

The other man mumbled something but it didn't

matter; von Arco was really talking to himself.

'Because I knew this would come one day.' He swept the blacked out horizon with his hand. 'This – the war. And it is war that the von Arcos are good at. You see, Hein, my family have always been soldiers. It is the only thing we know. How could we exist on that miserable potato field in East Prussia we call our home? So what have we been forced to do?' He gave a bitter laugh. 'Whether we have liked it or not the von Arcos have always gone to war to seek their fame and fortune – and sometimes to have our stupid turnips blown off.' He stopped abruptly, as if he had just realized what he had said.

A searchlight swept the anchorage. For an instant its icy white light illuminated von Arco's harsh, arrogant face. Hein shuddered. There was death written all over it . . .

In the smoke-filled cafés and whorehouses that lined the *fleets*, the canals which criss-crossed the harbour area, the men of the U-69 got drunk. They drank anything and everything, were sick, and began drinking again. What did it matter? Their life was fated to be short and brutal.

They drank and grew sad and sentimental. They drank and grew angry and pugnacious. Men clung around each other's necks and wept openly, while the bloated, middle-aged whores stared at them unbelievingly. Men who were best friends thrashed at each other, using every dirty waterfront trick to put the other man down on the sawdust floor. Men staggered outside vomiting and howling at the moon like mad dogs. Men collapsed finally into blessed oblivion, young heads resting in pools of stale beer. Men attacked women like savage animals, ripping down their knickers, thrusting their legs open plunging themselves into the soft, yielding bodies, gasping and grunting in wild, bestial fury to collapse in the end like dead men. Men who were doomed to death trying to forget . . .

And as he walked back to his ship through the blacked-out streets patrolled by middle-aged *Schupos** operating in twos, ensign Jungblut listened to the drunken caterwauling, the screams and the raucous cries, and nodded his head in understanding. 'Poor little fishes,' he said sadly. 'Poor little fishes . . .'

* Policemen

CHAPTER 4

'Gentlemen, may I have your attention please!'

The chatter in the big operations room stopped immediately. The young U-boat skippers in their number one uniforms, some of them already bearing decorations for bravery in action, turned at once to face the rostrum. For a moment there was silence broken only by the heavy stamp of the sentries pacing the gravel paths outside.

Karl Doenitz stared at them, that hard, flat face of his set and purposeful, but his eyes revealed his pride in these young officers. He had made them and he was proud of them. In the whole world there were no better U-boat skippers than these.

There was Prien, dapper and slim with a mild manner that hid a stubborn, impetuous nature. He knew that Prien had a savagely biting wit with which he kept at bay any would-be friend. He hated invaders into his personal life. A loner, in short, who obtained results.

Schepke, standing next to him, was completely the reverse. Tall and always cheerful, he possessed charm and blond good looks. Tough and forceful as he was, these two qualities were his downfall. He revelled in admiration and Doenitz knew from his own experiences as a U-boat commander in the Old War that a captain could not afford to be popular. Still, a very good man.

Then there was Kretschmar, perhaps the toughest of the three younger skippers. The twenty-four-year-old skipper lived for the sea; it was his only love. Doenitz told himself that Kretschmar was like he had been when young. He had a cruel contempt for weakness in others. He possessed a bigoted refusal to allow ordinary human failings to interfere with duty. And he had the confident bearing of a man who, although young, knew what he was doing. Doenitz frowned suddenly. The handsome young officer had just lit another black cigar. Over the first few months of the war Kretschmar had become a chain smoker of the damned things. Did that mean a weakness? Was he suffering from nerves already? Doenitz turned his gaze on the oldest skipper there that morning, Lt. Commander Hanssen. He knew Hanssen of old. He was tough, he was blunt - even outspoken - and he was witty in a way that went down well with his crews. None of the skippers present this day were liked - not to say loved - as much by their crews as Hanssen was. But was Hanssen ruthless enough, that was the problem? This business with von Arco and the machine-gunning of the Tommy sailors showed that Hanssen, the most experienced skipper there, still clung to the outmoded chivalry of the old days. But to succeed in this war a skipper needed to be icy-hearted and completely ruthless. Could Hanssen be like that when he needed to be?

Doenitz spoke. 'Gentlemen, time is running out. Already we know from radio intercepts that the Tommy ships the *Hood* and the *Renown* have left Scapa Flow. An unidentified aircraft-carrier has also sailed. It seems to us that that drunken sot Churchill is slowly breaking up the Home Fleet. If we do not strike soon the bird will have flown.'

'Some bird, sir!' Schepke commented in his usual easy fashion. 'Half a million tons of the biggest fleet in the world. Some bird!'

'Exactly, Schepke,' Doenitz answered while the others stared at him intently, almost fiercely, not even smiling at Schepke's attempt to defuse the tautness of the conference. 'So if we are going to gain some sort of kudos for the U-boat arm and show those damned stubble-hoppers of the Army that *we* are also fighting this war we must act – and act *soon*!'

Inwardly Hanssen grinned. 'Kudos for the U-boat arm,' he told himself. Kudos for Doenitz was what he meant. The man was a born glory-hunter. He waited for his cue.

It came: 'Commander Hanssen, please report on your reconnaissance of last week.'

Hanssen stepped forward smartly and posted himself in front of the huge map of Northern Europe. Briskly and very professionally he related the details of the U-69's penetration of Scapa Flow, while the others listened intently. 'In short, comrades,' he concluded, 'an attack on Scapa Flow is viable. It appears that the British have no secret weapon to defend their ships in the anchorage as we had previously feared and that their defence is limited to the old World War One boom.' He looked at Doenitz enquiringly.

Doenitz nodded and snapped, 'Thank you, Commander.'

Hanssen strode back to his place.

Doenitz waited a while and let Hanssen's words sink in before saying, 'Now the only questions are these: which channel shall we use for our attack . . ?' He paused momentarily, knowing that this was the most important question of all for these brave young skippers eager for some desperate glory. 'And *who* will carry out that attack?'

That second question fell among them like a bombshell. Doenitz could feel their excitement almost physically. Prien's eyes blazed. Kretschmar leaned forward, gaze devouring Doenitz' face as if he were willing him to name him. Even Schepke's normally good-humoured, handsome face had grown tense and anxious as if he could not bear to be turned down. Only Hanssen's witty blue eyes revealed nothing, save perhaps a hint of contempt. Doenitz frowned. Did Hanssen disapprove of this sort of thing? What was going through *his* mind? He cleared his throat and continued.

'Let us tackle the first problem, the question of which channel should be used,' he announced, picking up a pointer and gazing up at the map. 'Holm in the east, Hoxa in the south or Hoy in the west?'

'I have sailed the Fair Isle Passage leading to Hoxa, sir,' Kretschmar ventured. 'I would opt for Hoxa.'

His face revealing nothing, Doenitz told himself that Kretschmar had just lost the race. He was too eager. 'Wrong, Kretschmar,' he snapped like a schoolmaster putting down some teacher's pet. 'Hoxa is out for three reasons. One: the strongest cross-currents in British coastal waters are to be found there. Two: aerial reconnaissance has now shown that it is the most heavily guarded entrance of the three. Three: it is the principal gateway for Tommy warships entering and leaving the anchorage.'

Schepke tittered softly at Kretschmar's discomfiture and the latter blushed. Doenitz waited.

Prien tried. 'Which entrance have you selected, sir?' he asked simply and Doenitz knew he had found his captain. Hanssen did too. Prien had just won the flower vase. He had asked exactly the right question in the right manner. It would mean the Knight's Cross and glory for *Oberleutnant* Prien. '*And an early death*!' said a hoarse, mocking voice at the back of his head. But Commander Hanssen ignored that particular prophet of doom.

'My staff have considered the question carefully, Prien,' Doenitz answered. 'They – and I – have come to the conclusion that Holm in the east is the most weakly defended entrance.' He tapped the map with his pointer. 'The aerial photographs show that the entrance is split into three channels by two small islands. With a bit of luck a U-boat could penetrate one of those channels. But it is going to be tricky,' Doenitz warned. 'The U-boat would have to navigate a channel of nearly two kilometres in length with less than twelve metres' clearance on both sides and in rough water no deeper than ten metres.' He stopped suddenly, waiting for their reaction.

It came quickly. Prien whistled softly. Kretschmar sucked his front teeth loudly and Schepke said, 'You could get a nasty case of arse-ache in a channel like that. Not to mention your head when the Tommies start dropping square eggs on top of it. No U-boat could hide in that depth of water.'

'By night it could,' Doenitz replied softly.

Even Hanssen gasped. The channel sounded bad, even in the poor light provided by the periscope during daylight hours. But to do it at night. *Himmelherrje*, that was virtually suicidal! Suddenly the whole op went sour on him. This was going to be an Ascension Day command* by the looks of it and he wanted no part of that kind of op!

Doenitz didn't seem to notice. 'The boat picked,' he continued, 'will sail submerged for twenty-four hours. It will enter the channel at slack water time, wait for the tide to turn and then 'stern' through the channel against the tide, both on entering *and* leaving.'

'If there is any "leaving",' the small voice in Hanssen's head commented cynically.

'Now what is left of the British Home Fleet in the sound?' Doenitz answered his own question. 'As of yesterday, according to aerial reconnaissance, there are one aircraft carrier, five heavy ships, possibly battleships, and ten cruisers.' He paused, seeing the greedy look which had appeared in the eyes of his skippers.

'Christ!' Schepke exclaimed, his previous doubts forgotten instantly. 'Sink that little lot and we'd win enough tin to sink my good old U-23! *All those fat cats*!'

There was a murmur of agreement from the others as they visualized those tempting targets, every one at anchor and completely defenceless against an underwater attack. It would be a great slaughter.

* A one way mission i.e. suicidal

Hanssen thought of that day, in what now seemed another age, when he had sailed with the rest of the German Grand Fleet to surrender to the Tommies at Scapa Flow. He shivered suddenly, a mixture of emotion and pride. It would be the ideal retribution – to sink the pride of the Royal Navy as they lay at anchorage.

'So now, comrades,' Doenitz continued, 'let us get down to practicalities. It is obvious that there is only going to be one boat to get through that narrow channel. The question now . . .'

As one, the young skippers clicked to attention, and stepping one pace forward smartly, they cried, '*Sir, I volunteer my ship and crew!*'

Doenitz gave them a wintry smile. His pride and pleasure were only too obvious. 'I thank you comrades. But still the problem remains. One U-boat only.' He looked at Prien. '*Oberleutnant zur See* Prien,' he announced very formally. 'Your U-47 will have the task of entering the sound.'

A heavy silence descended abruptly on the big operations room. Hanssen, perhaps the only U-boat skipper there at that moment not affected by Doenitz' announcement, could feel that almost claustrophobic atmosphere, a mixture of anger, chagrin and resentment. For a moment it almost seemed that Schepke might well protest. Hanssen could see how his bottom lip trembled like that of a schoolboy on the verge of tears. Kretschmar, for his part, clenched his fists in the pockets of his tunic and glared at Prien, his eyes smouldering with suppressed rage.

Cold-blooded and unemotional as he was, Doenitz was well aware what prima donnas his U-boat skippers were and he said hastily, 'There will be glory enough to go round comrades. You all have a part to play in this great operation, which I will detail later. But first we will drink a toast to its success.' He clapped his hands loudly.

Almost as if they had been listening outside, the two high

doors swung open and two immaculate stewards entered bearing silver trays lined with chilled glasses of *aquavit*. Speedily and efficiently they passed a glass of fiery white spirit to each of the young skippers who now faced Doenitz, their minds racing as they wondered what their part would be in the coming op.

Doenitz took his glass and raised it to the third button of his tunic his arm set at a rigid angle as naval regulations prescribed. 'Gentlemen,' he barked, 'I wish you to drink a toast with me.' As one they brought their glasses up. 'To revenge, gentlemen. In memory of the disgrace of 1918.' For a moment his cold eyes blazed as they caught Hanssen who knew what he meant by disgrace. '*REVENGE*!'

'*REVENGE*!' they cried lustily, young faces blazing with the excitement of that old atavatistic, teutonic fury.

In one they drained the *aquavit*.

Next instant glass after glass shattered against the marble framework of the huge fireplace in a furious barrage. The die had been cast . . . They were going in . . .

CHAPTER 5

It was a very busy time for Christian Jungblut. While the shipwrights at the great Howaldt Works, located on the Elbe, worked full out, three shifts a day, to repair the battered U-69 and meet Doenitz' schedule, von Arco kept him running back and forth across the great port, obtaining munitions and supplies for the craft. New torpedoes were secured, electrically powered and equipped with magnetic detonators. A 2 cm anti-aircraft gun was going to be mounted on the boat and so ammunition for this new calibre cannon, plus that for the existing 88mm cannon, had to be requsitioned. Food - great smoked hams, salami sausages, salt beef halves, mountains of cans of all shapes and sizes and contents - had to be procured. As Frensen exclaimed as he saw the mountains of cans being deposited on the quayside, 'God in heaven, sir, how will I know which can has got the pussy in it!' Christian had laughed at the old sailor's joke and doubled off to yet another warehouse to demand fresh supplies; for von Arco had ordered severely, 'We must have enough food and supplies aboard, Ensign Jungblut, to last us for eight weeks!'

An eight weeks patrol! he had thought to himself and whistled softly. Where in the three devils' name were they going for two whole months? But he asked no questions, for as Frensen had put it to him, glancing at the new temporary-Skipper von Arco as he had stalked back and forth proudly with his inevitable check-board in hand,

'When the king says crap, sir, bend and take the strain, for in these days the word of the king is law.' And he had spat contemptuously into the dirty water below. Christian Jungblut had got the point.

Still, as much as he now disliked von Arco, just as everyone else in the crew did, he *did* admire his efficiency and his determination to have the boat ready for the mysterious mission for which it was intended. He spared himself not at all; chivvying, harassing, threatening, cajoling crew and civilian workers alike to get the job done, rushing back and forth all day long, face set with a fanatical will, crying over and over again, '*Dalli . . . dalli . . . los . . . los* . . . Let's get it done . . . *Dalli . . . dalli*!'

By the end of the day, most of the crew were too exhausted to leave the sailors' home in which they were billeted across the Elbe from the shipwright's yard. Only a few of the tougher members of the crew, such as Frensen and Maydag, seemed able to summon up enough energy to depart for the dubious pleasures of the *Reeperbahn*, with its gaudy music halls and shady brothels.

Christian too, tired as he was by the time evening arrived, was not going to be deprived of the sights and pleasures of Germany's greatest port before he was incarcerated in the 'tin coffin', as the crew had cynically dubbed the U-69, for what looked like eight weeks. He forced himself to shave and shower, change into his number one uniform, now proudly bearing the submariner's badge, and disappear into the hustle and bustle of the city.

In spite of the war, Hamburg enjoyed itself. The cafés, the clubs, the cinemas might well be blacked-out after dark, but they pulsated with life. Well-dressed businessmen, party officials and elegant naval staff officers were everywhere, escorting the cool northern blondes of the area, who kept Christian's heart beating excitedly all the time. Of course, he did not have the kind of money on an ensign's pay to frequent the plush hotels such as the

Vierjahrszeiten or the *Atlantik*, both on the Alster, the city's inner lake, where such unattached females could be found. Yet it was almost pleasure enough to watch them, tall and elegant, with those cool blue eyes, as they sat over their *Kaffee und Kuchen* in the little cafés which fringed the *Jungfernstieg* and the fashionable *Monckebergstrasse*. Sometimes he would sit hunched over a beer in such places for hours, just barely able to contain himself, heart in his mouth, staring at one of those desirable creatures being spoiled by a rich middle-aged businessman who was obviously going to bed her that night.

Of course it was grossly unfair, he knew. Soon he would depart to risk his life for 'Folk, Fatherland, and Führer' while they would remain behind, enjoying their delightful pleasures, not even aware of the terrible dangers he was running for them. Yet he accepted it as a fact of life. Was it not again that old bearded petty officer's 'sharks and little fishes' theory? One day, if he survived and returned a bemedalled hero, his face on the front page of the *Volkischer Beobachter*, the Führer's own newspaper, things would be different. Then he too would be a 'shark' and those cool blondes would be all over him, just begging him to 'dance the mattress polka' with them, as Petty Officer Frensen put it in his own bawdy fashion. Till that time he would just have to watch and wait.

But Ensign Christian Jungblut was not fated to sail on his first combat mission without sampling the delights of one of those cool northern blondes. Soon young Christian would have his pleasure – and for the first time in his young life be confronted with the harsh realities of the regime for which he was still prepared to sacrifice his life . . .

Frensen and his running-mate Maydag had no problems in finding companions for the night – save one: the money they needed to buy the whores who crowded the *Reeperbahn's*

Grosse Freiheit, *Moulin Rouge*, and the *Hippodrom* was rapidly beginning to run out. As Frensen said mournfully to Maydag as they sat in the *Hippodrom* watching whores cantering around the circle of sawdust on horseback, 'Old house, I've got enough Marie* for a good old roger tonight and that's it, shipmate. I'm skinned!'

Maydag took his eyes off a great beast of a whore who was riding past on a panting, gasping pony which looked as if it might collapse at any moment under her weight, and said, 'Well, I need me nooky regular, that's for sure.'

'Now then, what have we got that them civvies ain't got?' Frensen plodded on ignoring his shipmate's comment. 'Let me ask yer that.'

The fat whore fell from the sway-backed nag to reveal a great mass of pale flesh adorned with black garters, while the nag limped gasping to the side of the ring. 'Well, I don't know about you,' Maydag said thickly, eyeing all that blubber, 'but *I've* got a hard-on, if that's what you mean.'

'Stow it!' Frensen snapped. 'Try to be frigging serious, won't yer, you little arse-with-ears! Now what we've got is this: we've got *real coffee beans*, and all them whores has got is *ersatz* – thin-piss which goes under the name of "*mucki fuck*".† That's what we've got.' He sat back grandly and eyed with some interest a young blonde smoking a black cigar who was now trying to mount one of the long-suffering ponies. He saw almost immediately, however, that she was not a true blonde. Still, she'd be worth a half a kilo of real coffee beans any day.

'We ain't got real coffee beans,' Maydag protested, looking at him suspiciously. 'The Quartermaster's got them. We only get that kind of first class stuff – chocs and the like – when we're on ops.'

'Bird-brain!' Frensen snorted impatiently. 'But we're

* Money
† Trade name of a coffee substitute made of acorns

soon gonna be on ops, ain't we? Young Ensign Jungblut is requisitioning that kind of lovely grub all the time.'

'Aye, but we're not Jungblut,' Maydag objected.

The blonde was mounted now and cantering around the sawdust ring with her hair streaming behind her and her beautiful breasts, unrestrained by a bra, bobbing up and down like two delicious ripe melons. Frensen licked his lips as if in anticipation of the feast to come.

'Well?' Maydag persisted. 'Piss or get off the pot. What yer got on yer mind?'

'This.' Frensen forgot the braless blonde. 'We nick a requisition form from that arsehole von Arco's locker and you apply yer cunning little flipper to it – to the tune of, say, ten kilos of coffee. That should keep us in hot, steaming female gash until we sail.'

'Apply me flipper . . . *to do what*?' Maydag asked cautiously.

'Grow up, apeturd, willya!' Frensen said. 'Why, to forge young Jungblut's signature, that's what.'

In the ring the blonde decided to ride side-saddle. Naturally that way she could display her wares to the admiring sailors and civilians better. Frensen caught a delightful glimpse of black pubic hair. 'Get a load of that, Maydag,' he groaned as if in utter despair. 'All that lovely beaver – it's parted in the middle too – and it's all going to waste because we ain't got them real coffee beans . . .'

Maydag gave in. He crossed his wrists like a criminal surrendering to the police handcuffs. 'All right, Frensen, you've convinced me. But if we ever get caught out with our knickers down, mate, that frigging aristocratic streak o' piss von Arco'll swing us by the neck from the nearest yard-arm!'

The sirens began their sad wail just as Christian was crossing from the *Spitalstrasse* in the direction of the *Hauptbahnhof*, its entrance decorated with the inevitable poster, bold red letters announcing that '*WHEELS ROLLED FOR VICTORY*.' Almost immediately the steel-helmeted wardens started to shrill their whistles officiously and here and there military policemen patrolling the station began to shout, 'This way, people! This way to the shelters. Remember you are German, don't panic . . . This way!'

'Yes,' a tough Hamburg voice replied from the darkness, 'but do them shitting buck-teethed Tommies know we are?'

Nobody laughed.

Suddenly Christian found himself being pressed forward by a throng of nervous civilians: old grannies dragging heavy baskets, excited young women trying to catch the last trains to the port's surburbs, a handful of drunks and the usual hangers-on one found outside big stations everywhere. He tried to fight his way clear. He had no intention of spending half the night in some stale shelter, heavy with smell of sweat and the acrid odour of the 'piss-buckets' which were the only form of sanitation. But the throng was too tight and abruptly he found himself thrust close to a tall blonde who he could see in the dim blue lights of the MPs' torches was one of those Nordic beauties of his dreams.

'What a mix-up!' he exclaimed as they were pushed and shoved closer to the entrance of the shelter, guarded by two officious middle-aged wardens in steel helmets who were examining everyone's *Ausweis* as they entered.

'Mix-up is the word for it!' she replied in the flat quick accent of the coast, though there was no warmth in her voice. Instead Christian imagined he could detect a note of alarm in it. Was she scared?

Now she was just in front of Christian, who fumbled with his own ID. He could overlook the stench of the shelter in the presence of such a delightful creature. But that was not to be.

The taller of the two wardens examined the girl's papers in the blue light of the torch clipped to his breast pocket, while behind, the others thrust forward, eager to be inside before the bombs started to fall. Suddenly he grunted, 'Take off, Sarah. We don't want your kind in there polluting our good German air!'

'But . . .' the blonde began tearfully.

'No buts! On your way!' the big warden interrupted brutally. 'You're lucky that I am not reporting you to the police for trying to pull a damned trick like that. *Move it*!'

Christian grabbed the surprised warden by the lapels and almost jerked him off his feet. 'What a way to talk to a lady!' he cried angrily as the flak began to thunder to the west. 'Why shouldn't she enter the shelter like the rest of us, you damned *Schweinhund*?'

'But sir,' the warden protested, recognising Christian's uniform with the golden badge of the active submariner on the breast, 'It is orders sir . . . right from the top . . . From Berlin . . . Her kind cannot be allowed to enter. They have to find their own source of shelter. Can't you see?'

Christian shook his head grimly. 'No, I can't damnwell see! What are you rabbiting on about?'

'This, sir!' the other warden said flashing his torch on the white-faced girl.

Jungblut caught a glimpse of a beautiful oval face, framed by that long white-blonde hair, and then the blue beam fell lower to the lapel of her white *staubmantel*, the typical dust-coat that Hamburg women were wearing that summer.

Christian gasped and slowly very slowly relinquished his grasp on the taller of the two wardens. There, clearly illuminated by the blue light, was a badge: a familiar five-pointed star painted in dull gold on her lapel. It was the Star of David.

The cool nordic blonde was a Jewess!

CHAPTER 6

'I had a bit of the other on a hillside once,' Frensen said casually, as the fat, bald-headed old quartermaster peered at the list of supplies through his nickel-rimmed glasses. 'Hard graft, I can tell yer, Quartermaster. Screwing uphill! But finally I got me bearings. I swung her arse round one hundred and eighty degrees to port and really banged her till her glassy orbits nearly popped!'

The naval quartermaster laughed so much that his heavy jowls slapped together audibly. 'You're a card, *Obermaat*,' he chortled, pencil poised in the air ready to check off another item of the requisition list. At the window, Maydag watched anxiously. Frensen was trying to blind the fat old fool with bullshit. He only hoped it worked; otherwise it would be the brig for both of them.

'At my age, *Obermaat*,' the Quartermaster said, 'I prefer them on top. You know.' He thrust out his pudgy hands as if he were balancing a woman on his ample middle. 'Not so much hard work for me. Let the gash do the hard graft. Walk, trot, canter, *gallop*, if you follow me, *Obermaat*.' He winked.

Frensen nodded that he did. 'You've got a wicked way with the wenches, Quartermaster,' he said heartily. 'I bet you could tell some juicy stories if you wanted to.'

The Quartermaster frowned suddenly. 'Ten kilos of bean coffee?' he exclaimed.

Maydag tensed. Frensen pretended not to hear. He looked out of the barred window of the stores as if bored, softly singing a dirty ditty of his own composition: '*There limped through the burning Sahara . . . a poor syphilitic old whore . . . Old Sheikh Abdul whipped out his red-hot banana . . . and soon she was begging for more . . .*'

'But you've had your special combat ration of bean coffee,' the Quartermaster persisted.

Frensen pretended to hear for the first time. 'You said something, Quartermaster?'

'Yes, I said that you'd already had your ration of bean coffee.'

Frensen shrugged easily, though inside he was tense. If they were caught they'd really be for the high jump. 'You know officers, Quartermaster. As one noncom to another, officers don't know their arse from their elbow. Besides, the officer who indented for the goodies is our Moses. Young Ensign Jungblut. Nice young feller but as green as growing corn.' He dismissed the matter. 'Hurry it up, old house, willyer. We've only got two more days in port, and me and that asparagus Tarzan over there has got a couple of hot numbers laid on for this afternoon.' He winked knowingly. 'Mine's a contortionist. They say she can do it with her legs wrapped round the back of her head! I can't wait to give her a taste of the old salami.' He grabbed the front of his trousers urgently.

'Oh well, if that's the case I'll pass it. But I'd better note the name of the officer.' Laboriously he began to write Jungblut's name down on his pad while behind him Maydag wiped the thin film of sweat from his brow. They'd pulled it off! They'd be walking on female tits – right up to the ankles – for the rest of their time in Hamburg!

Christian Jungblut, whose name was being recorded at that very moment, watched with little interest as one of the old salts carefully bored holes in the soles of his shoes with a red-hot needle. 'You see, Ensign,' he said, 'When you're on watch, you wear your escape suit, our only link with the world – besides the speaking tube. But don't imagine the damn thing is waterproof! The stuff always seeps through it in the end and the trouble is that the suit at the bottom is so thick that water can't run out. So it starts to climb higher and higher up your legs till sometimes it reaches your guts. Imagine standing a whole watch with icy sea water floating around yer eggs! A man could lose something very precious, like,' he said with some indignation. 'Your outside plumbing could freeze up something horrid. So that's why we bore holes into our shoes, to let the water run off.'

Christian nodded his head in understanding, but his gaze remained fixed on the green tower of the *Michaeliskirche*, only one minute from where she lived in the cellar. Paula Petersen she was called, tall, blonde and Nordic, straight from the school textbooks illustrating the ideal German as visualized by the crackpot, racial purists of the Third Reich. 'Yes,' she had said, a faint smile on her beautiful face as they had pushed their way through the throng outside the shelter, 'I'm not at all what you would expect of a Jewess am I, *Herr Leutnant*?'

'*Ensign*,' he had corrected her hastily as they had stepped out into the black-out, the searchlights parting the clouds with silver fingers, looking for the Tommy bombers. 'Ensign Christian Jungblut.'

They had shaken hands formally as if this were peacetime and they had been just introduced at some bourgeois tea-party. To the west, the guns rolled. The Tommies were coming. 'Dark, small, hook-nosed and servile, that's what those brown bully boys of the Party expect us to be. Pathetically grateful to be still alive and allowed enough rations to survive on,' she had said as he steered her across the street in the direction of the church.

'I'm sorry,' he had blurted out unwittingly.

'Sorry for what?' She had rounded on him, her blue eyes bold and challenging in the reflected light of the search-lights. 'I don't mind being a Jewess - *now*!' She had not qualified that 'now' and he had not dared ask what it meant. He didn't want to lose her just after he had met her. 'In fact, I am rather proud of being one. Better than being one of those cruel pot-bellied perverts in their brown uniforms who call themselves Germans.' A minute or two later they had shaken hands again formally and she had slipped into the cellar in which she apparently lived alone (her parents had already fled to America just before the outbreak of war), leaving him to walk back to his quarters through the deserted, blacked-out streets, his young mind in a turmoil.

Now sitting in the thin autumn sunshine some twenty hours later, listening to the sailor talking, Christian was seized by an overwhelming longing to see Paula Petersen again. There was nothing to stop him doing so - he was off duty for the next six hours and his own personal kit was in order, ready for sailing once the refit was finished - save for one thing: he was a naval officer in uniform and she was a Jewess wearing that Star of David. Suddenly he flushed and was angry with himself for even having thought of that particular problem. He wanted to see her again - and damn the Star of David!

'Of course, we all get rheumatics in the end. In the U-boat Service,' the old salt was saying bitterly, 'we're all cripples by the time we're thirty-odd. It's all that freezing salt water, Ensign you see . . .' He looked up and stopped short. Ensign Jungblut was gone.

'You know what they say, mates,' the big petty officer sneered, 'that lot in the U-69 make love with their mouths. That's why they call it the *sixty-nine*! Get it, mates?' He made a sucking sound with his pursed lips and the line of petty officers waiting to enter the brothel, although it was still only mid-day, laughed in a good-humoured manner.

Frensen gave a polite little smile. 'Did someone here fire the old fart-cannon, Maydag?' he enquired mildly. 'There's an awful lot o' green smoke about. Or do yer think it's somebody off'n the U-47? They're allus crapping their skivvies.'

The big petty officer who had spoken flushed angrily, doubling his fists like small steam-shovels. 'How do you know I'm from Lieutenant Prien's boat?' he demanded, thrusting his brutal brick-red face into Frensen's. '*Eh?*'

Frensen drew back slipping on his brass knuckles behind his back, and giggled in a fake falsetto. 'Oh, don't come so close, you naughty sailor, you'll give me my monthlies in a moment . . . *Cos you stink, you arse-with-ears*!' he cried, reverting to his normal deep bass. 'That's why. Want to make anything of it.'

'Another peep outa you, shiteheel, and yer'll be lacking a set o' teeth!' the man from the U-47 threatened.

Behind Frensen, Maydag clutched the precious sack of real coffee beans to his skinny chest like a mother cradling her only child, mind racing desperately for a solution to the quarrel. In a minute the situation would explode and they'd never get inside the brothel, where already the rusty bedsprings were creaking tantalizingly from every bedroom.

'Oh dear me, you've frightened me,' Frensen simpered. 'I think I've peed down my right leg.'

'You'll be pissing through yer armpit by the time I've finished with yer if you don't knock it off!' the petty officer hissed through gritted teeth, raising his brawny right arm.

'Fart in the wind, shitehawk!' Frensen said easily, the brass knuckles firmly fixed on his right fist now.

'Mates,' Maydag said desperately. 'Can't we knock it off? They'll be letting us in soon. And listen to that lovely music coming from upstairs. They're going at it like a frigging fiddler's elbow!'

The man from the U-47 looked down at Maydag. 'You'll be next,' he said simply. 'After I've torn the flippers off that big mate of yours.' He leapt forward, fists swinging. Frensen braced his feet and popped out his right, straight ahead. The cruelly mailed fist caught the other petty officer right on the chin. 'Ouch,' he said, quite gently. He came to a dead stop. His eyes revolved strangely. A stupid, idiotic grin spread across his big face. It was almost as if he were drunk. His knees began to give. Gently, very gently, he sank to the pavement, out to the world.

'Hey, that frigger from the sixty-nine's wearing brass knuckles!' an indignant voice cried. 'That ain't fair, mates.'

'Nothing's fair in love and war, mates,' Frensen chortled in high good humour as the heavy steel gas-mask case slammed into the back of his shaven skull, sending him reeling against the wall groggily.

'Why, you rotten treacherous bastard!' Maydag cried indignantly. Still clutching his precious beans to his skinny chest, he lashed out with his foot.

The boot caught the sailor who had hit Frensen right in the crotch. He went reeling back, clutching his injured testicles, vomiting and choking. 'He's ruined my love-machine . . . my love-machine is smashed . . .'

That did it. In an instant men were fighting each other everywhere, rolling in the gutter, slamming one another against the walls, reeling back and forth across that sordid *Herbertstrasse*,* littered with used contraceptives, while the half-naked whores leaned out of their windows cheering them on happily.

Whistles shrilled. There was the screech of hurrying tyres. Brakes howled and then there they were: half a

* A notorious street of brothels in Hamburg

hundred helmeted naval police falling from their trucks, carbines and clubs at the ready.

'*Shore patrol!*' someone yelled.

The mêlée parted as if by magic. Maydag grabbed Frensen's arm. 'Come on wood-head! Let's get us out of here. Hindlegs in yer hands shipmate!'

But it was already too late. Five big cops, clubs at the ready, were advancing upon them, determination written all over their ugly mugs. In the lead came a huge petty officer balancing a carbine in his hand as if it were a kid's toy. With his other he was beckoning to the two comrades, a happy, understanding smile on his tough face. 'Come to daddy, you naughty boys,' he was saying gently. 'Come on now . . . make daddy happy. He's going to take you for walkies and then he'll have a nice supper of bread and water prepared for you . . . Come along now. Don't keep daddy waiting.'

Maydag's heart sank to his boots, the coffee beans still clutched to his chest which was burning now like fire. They had been nabbed, well and truly nabbed. Now it was Swedish curtains for them for sure.* Tamely he allowed himself to be led to the waiting police truck.

* Naval slang for prison bars

CHAPTER 7

'*Juden raus . . . Juden raus . . . Kaufe nicht bei Juden Volksgenossen . . . Juden heraus . . !*'

Christian frowned as he heard the monotonous cries and saw the fat middle-aged brown-shirt parading up and down before the line of miserable Jewish shops advising his 'people's comrades' not to buy their pathetic wares. As he passed Christian, he saluted quite stiffly and an unhappy Christian was forced to return the salute.

Paula was standing in the doorway of a dirty, shabby little shop, its window cracked and smeared with years of anti-Jewish slogans, comforting an old man in carpet slippers who had been crying. 'There there, Herr Rosengarten,' she was saying soothingly. 'They won't harm you any more.' She looked into the dark, smelly interior where the only goods still for sale were a pile of ruined cabbages, now dripping with the stale urine that a gang of Hitler Youth kids had poured over them five minutes before. 'You've got nothing more to sell.'

'Thank you, *Fraulein* Petersen, you are very kind,' the old man wheezed and then he hobbled back into his shop, shaking his white head as if he couldn't believe the evidence of his own faded eyes. '*Meschugge*,' he muttered, 'the whole world's *meschugge* . . .'

'*Frauline* Petersen,' Christian said hesitantly.

She turned, startled, and he raised his hand to his cap in salute. 'It's you,' she said simply. 'My ensign.'

His heart leapt with joy. '*Your* ensign?'

'It's only a manner of speech,' she smiled. 'But come on. Let me take you into my humble home. I don't think it would do your career much good to be seen with me. Those brown-shirted pigs,' she indicated the man with the hoarding suspended from his shoulders at the end of the street, 'report everything to the Gestapo.'

Five minutes later the two of them were seated in her 'humble home', a tight cellar with peeling wallpaper and smelling of damp, sipping herbal tea and chatting excitedly as if they had known each other all their young lives.

'I was a fool not to go with my parents while I still had time,' she explained, her beautiful pale face relaxed for the first time. 'But somehow I thought things would change – even after they slung me out of high school. You know what they say – the soup is never eaten as hot as it is cooked.'

He nodded, entranced by her beauty, and let her talk. From outside came the stamp of heavy jackboots and that monotonous cry, '*Juden raus . . . Juden raus . . .*'

'In a way I thought my parents were like the proverbial rats abandoning the ship. Fleeing for their lives so that they could open a kosher delicatessen in Brooklyn.' She giggled as though it was funny. 'Now what can I do? They won't let me go to the university. I can't train for anything. It's hard.'

'But what do you do?' he asked. 'How do you live.'

'Do?' She looked at him boldly. 'Anything! Everything! But not *that* yet. At least *not* for money.'

Christian flushed and impulsively she pressed his hand and laughed. 'I'm in limbo. Waiting in an eternal fourth-class railway waiting room. It's a strange existence, living from hand to mouth, from day to day. *Nothing* matters. *Everything* matters. The smell of the Elbe at the *Landungsbrucke* . . . The *lap-lap* of the water on the Alster . . . The cry of the gulls . . . It's my city too, you know, Hamburg . . .'

Suddenly his heart went out to her and he knew he was

in love for the first time in his young life. He touched her hand softly and nodded.

Abruptly her blue eyes flushed with tears. 'Oh my God, how I wish I was like everybody else! Twenty years old in 1939, concerned only with my hair, whether I had enough points for another dress, if my boyfriend thought that my breasts were big enough . . . Simple things. Not concerned with world-shaking events . . .' Her voice dropped and she bent her head, her long blonde hair hiding her face and muffling what she had to say. 'Not worrying all the time about how much longer they'll let me live . . .'

Outside, the heavy boots stamped by once more. '*Juden raus*,' that harsh brutal voice demanded yet again. '*Juden raus . . .*'

The fat old Gestapo man moved his unlit stump of cigar from one side of his mouth to the other, his green leather coat creaking with the effort. 'Jailbait,' he announced. 'Real jailbait, *Herr Oberleutnant*.'

Next to him, both handcuffed and looking the worse for wear, Maydag and Frensen glared, while von Arco looked suitably tough. He had never liked either of them. This was his chance, he told himself.

'Ten pounds or more of bean coffee we found on the little prick,' the fat Gestapo man went on, 'before we tumbled to the fact that he was trying to ditch it. *Real bean coffee*,' he added significantly.

'For the black market?' von Arco asked.

The Gestapo man nodded and worked his cigar from one side of his slack sensualist's mouth to the other once again. 'Sure.'

Von Arco tapped the requisition-form and the paper he had obtained from the quartermaster's office. 'Ensign Jungblut signed for that coffee among other things,' he said. 'What have you rogues to say about that, eh?'

Neither spoke. Their sullen faces revealed nothing but behind that façade both their minds raced alarmingly. If they confessed they had forged Jungblut's signature, it would be much worse for them; if they didn't, the U-69's 'Moses' would be for the high jump.

Von Arco looked at them grimly and the old Gestapo man said, 'Once we get them back to the station, *Herr Oberleutnant*, I'll see they talk. They say,' he looked modestly at the knuckles of his fat right hand, 'that old Schmitz can make even a mummy talk. They'll sing like canaries!'

'But I don't know how Ensign Jungblut got involved in this nasty business. And where in three devils' name is the young fool anyway?' said von Arco.

Standing next to the table, the Chief Petty Officer, who was looking sorrowfully at Frensen and Maydag, two of the U-69's best crewmen, said quickly, 'He has another thirty minutes off-duty, sir. He signed the log for this time.'

'I see. Then what are we going to do with them, Herr Schmitz?'

'*I shall tell you, von Arco.*'

Frensen gave an inner sigh of relief at that familiar cool voice. Next to him Maydag gulped.

Immediately von Arco sprang up and clicked to the position of attention while the fat Gestapo man stared in some bewilderment at the new arrival: a small, stocky civilian with deep-blue, witty eyes. 'What . . . what's going on?' he stuttered.

Captain Hanssen ignored him. 'Where's the fire?' he asked easily.

Hastily von Arco told him, wondering all the while what had brought Hanssen to Hamburg at this time of the evening.

Hanssen nodded several times before turning to face the two prisoners. '*Women?*' he demanded. 'It was whores. That's why you needed the coffee. Go on – spit it out!'

Maydag nodded and Frensen said, 'Yes sir, that's it. We'd run out of Marie . . . er . . . money and it was the only way we could get our oats. There was only two days left and we thought . . .' His voice trailed away to nothing as Hanssen turned to face the Gestapo man.

'The shore patrol handed the prisoners over to you?' he asked, voice without emotion.

The Gestapo man swung his cigar from one side of his slack mouth to the other. 'That's right.'

'On what authority?'

'The Gestapo does not need authority, Commander,' he replied. There was a slightly puzzled look on his fat old lecher's face. No one questioned the Gestapo – at least no one who was sane. 'This is a serious black market offence. We intervened automatically.'

'Then you were wrong!' Hanssen snapped with an air of finality. 'Release the two of them to the custody of my CPO.* I shall deal with them myself.'

'But I can't do that!' he stuttered.

'Oh yes you can.' Hanssen's voice was harsh and hard now and brooked no refusal. 'Those two criminals there are soon going to be risking their necks, crooked as they may be, on the high seas while you undoubtedly will be pressing some office chair with your nice fat comfortable butt. Here *I* decide who is guilty or innocent. *Now beat it*!'

The shocked and crimson-faced Gestapo official 'beat it', mumbling furiously about 'insults' and 'consequences' but totally ignored by Hanssen who looked at von Arco and announced simply, 'The U-69 sails on the morning tide. *We're on ops* . . .'

Now while the civilian painters worked under the glare of flood-lights, the black-out thrown to the winds because of

* Chief Petty Officer

this emergency, the sweating, cursing crew of the U-69 loaded the precious supplies collected by Ensign Jungblut. As the hours passed supplies for eight weeks disappeared between the network of pipes, ducts and valves which filled the U-boat's interior. Even the control room was not exempted: huge smoked hams hung there now, filling the place with the smell of the *rauchkammer*.* On shore the naval bakers worked overtime and handcarts were trundled back and forth across the cobbles, bearing with them piles of fresh bread and packets of pumpernickel which were stowed in any still unoccupied cranny.

Now the finishing touches were put to their preparations. The wooden floors were fitted above their fourteen torpedoes leaving just enough room for the men to squirm over them to their bunks and the torpedo tubes. The painters knocked off and were handed a bottle of schnaps by Hanssen as a reward for their labours.

Enviously Frensen and Maydag watched as the happy civilians poured the fiery spirit down their throats, passing the bottle from man to man. But they knew there would be no spirits for them this night. Hanssen had ordered the charge against them removed from the charge sheet but he had warned them grimly afterwards: 'From now on you two are on my personal shit-list! Remember that, Frensen and Maydag. I'm gonna be on your crooked arses day and night. As of now, no alcohol and five lung torpedoes† a day per man – *perhaps*!'

With Christian, Hanssen had been kind and understanding. 'There'll be no enquiry, Jungblut, I've seen to that. My guess is that those two horned oxen Frensen and Maydag forged your name on the requisition. It has been done before and it will be done again no doubt. U-boat men are notoriously horny. It goes with the job. You'll learn. They'll do anything to get themselves into a

* Smoke chamber

† Cigarettes

woman's pants.' He paused and looked at the Ensign as if he were seeing him for the first time, noting the keen eyes, the tough jaw, the intrinsic decency of the handsome face, and nodded as if approving of what he saw. 'All right, go ashore and pack your duds. You'll register their contents, label them, and,' he paused, face abruptly grave, 'in case you don't return, they'll be sent on to your folks.'

'Yessir. Thank you, sir!' Christian had clicked to attention and was preparing to move off when Hanssen added, 'and by the way, *officially* I'm giving you an errand to run for me to the Naval *Kommandatura. Unofficially* I'm telling you to beat it and see your best girl for a couple of hours while you've still got time. Who knows?' He shrugged like a man who had made his peace with the world and started to clamber up the conning-tower once more.

Christian had stammered a happy 'Thank you, sir' and then he was running along the quayside full out . . .

In the candle-lit cellar, as it reeled and trembled under the impact of the Tommy bombs and while the flak cannon thundered, he put his arms round her and kissed her passionate, almost savagely.

Paula responded wildly and with an animal abandon that Christian had not expected from her, pressing her slim rounded stomach against his aching, desperate loins. Gasping fervently, they tumbled onto the ancient bed, its springs creaking in rusty protest. His eager tongue burrowed deep into her gasping mouth. His trembling hand followed the line of the silk stocking till it found the hot naked flesh, and the striving fingers touched the soft wetness they sought. She sighed.

Suddenly the war, the raid, the fact that they might both be dead before the month was out were forgotten. Only *they* mattered as they writhed back and forth on the crazily creaking wooden bed, sobbing for breath, uttering wild little cries.

Once a bomb dropped nearby. The whole cellar shivered with the impact. Their sweating, naked, entwined bodies were showered by a rain of falling plaster flakes. They did not notice. Their shadows, magnified gigantically by the wildly flickering yellow light of the candle, continued this fervent, frantic dance. Their fevered desire consumed them as if there had never been another love-making. Against the background of a world gone mad, two young people tried to give some meaning to their fleeting existence . . .

And in the quiet of his quarters, now that the U-69 was loaded and the crew had fallen into an exhausted sleep, Lt. Commander Hanssen sat in the circle of yellow light cast by the desk lamp and began to compose that old, old letter that began: *Dear Heidi, Helmut and Gerda. You will only be reading this if something has happened to me – and you know what that 'something' is. I do not want you to grieve for me. All I ask of you is that you never forget me when I am gone . . .*

BOOK THREE

Black Saturday

'A pity that only one was destroyed.'

Lt. Gunther Prien, October 1939

CHAPTER 1

On Tuesday 10th October 1939, at six hundred hours precisely, the crews of the three U-boats of the 'Wolf Pack' anchored off Kiel's *Tirpitz Quay* began to board their subs.

At the gangplank of the U-69, lying up next to Prien's U-47, with beyond Kretschmar's U-23, Ensign Jungblut searched the crew for bottles of schnaps; for from now onwards there would be no more alcohol drunk aboard the U-69. Razors were tossed overboard too, whenever they were found. From this moment till the day they returned, no one in the crew would shave. All the boat's fresh water would be conserved for cooking and drinking. 'No naked lights within fifty metres, Ensign!' a few of the crew cracked and breathed hard on him as if they wanted him to smell 'the flag', as they called the whiff of the previous night's alcohol. But for the most part the crew were silent and serious, even pensive. They knew what was to come.

At eight, as the gloom gave way to a typical grey autumn day, with wisps of fog intertwining between the ships and the land, the naval band appeared and began to play rousing marches to the accompaniment of jeers and catcalls from the assembled U-boat crews. The bandsmen were on a cushy number; they'd probably see the end of October 1939 and the U-boat men knew it. Their own fate was less certain.

At nine the staff officers appeared, all elegant blue uniforms, gleaming buttons and swinging lanyards – 'monkeys' perches', as the U-boat men called them contemptuously. Obviously the 'Big Lion' - Doenitz himself - was on his way to bid them goodbye. 'The condemned man ate a hearty breakfast!' Hanssen commented to von Arco in high good humour. 'Real red carpet treatment.'

Von Arco did not speak; he couldn't. This op was going to be a bitch and suddenly he was very afraid.

Ten minutes later Doenitz appeared, surrounded by staff officers and, von Arco noticed, followed by Neurath carrying his usual notebook to record his chief's precious words. But he was no longer interested in *Oberleutnant* Neurath. It did not even give him pleasure to know that he had cuckolded the pompous ass many a time. Now there was a huge gap between his world and that of those on shore. Those on the quayside had a good chance of living; those on the boats were condemned men. It was as simple as that.

'Comrades!' Doenitz' harsh voice echoed and re-echoed metallically round the wharves. 'You all know that you are serving in the finest and most effective service of our beloved Fatherland - the U-Boat Service. The destiny of our country lies in your hands. Prove yourself worthy of that trust. Today you set out to strike a mighty blow for Germany - one that will echo throughout the world! I know that you sense no fear. But let us always remember the motto of our service: *Go in and sink*! Comrades, I salute you all . . .'

Doenitz clicked to attention and the band began to blare out the *Deutschlandlied*, all clashing cymbals, the rattle of kettle-drums, the blast of brass. Christian Jungblut had heard that old anthem thousands of times but never had he experienced such a spine-tingling sensation at the sound of it as he did now. *They were going to war . . . they were going to war . . .*

'*Deutschland . . . Deutschland . . . über alles . . . in der Welt* . . .' they sang on the quayside. Already U-47 was sliding away in reverse. Kretschmar's U-23 followed. Fifty metres from the pier her Skipper ordered the submerged hydroplanes cleared. The diesels started. Slowly she started to follow Prien's boat. Now it was the turn of the U-69.

'Start diesels!' von Arco commanded. The long steel frame shuddered. Dark fumes escaped from the exhausts. The twin screws thrashed the dirty water into a foamy white. Hanssen saluted the crowd on the quayside. 'Both engines ahead!' von Arco ordered. 'Steer nine-five!'

The U-69 turned sharply to starboard. Her bow cleaved the water, heading towards the centre of the bay. The music began to fade. On the conning-tower, standing next to Hanssen, Christian flung one last look at the quayside. Already the crowd of staff officers were beginning to disperse, moving back to their offices in groups of two or three, probably looking forward to another cup of hot coffee after the ceremony on the cold quayside. There were two worlds: that of the 'rear-echelon stallions' and that of the 'front-swine'; but he would not have had their world for all the gold in the Berlin *Reichsbank. He was going to war at last*!

One hour later they entered the locks at Holtenau and manoeuvred their way into the North-East Sea Canal built by the Kaiser for the day-long trip that would take them to the North Sea - and the enemy.

At ten o'clock on the morning of Wednesday 11th October they emerged from the Canal at Brunsbuettelkoog. Prien's U-47 took the lead of the Wolf Pack, with the other two submarines sailing in line and the U-69 bringing up the rear. Soon the shore-line sank beneath the smudgy horizon and a thin, grey, bitter rain set in.

On the bridge Hanssen frowned. 'Damned awful weather,' he complained, huddling deeper into his shining oilskin.

'Give us good air cover, sir,' Frensen said, peering at the dull, overcast sky with his big binoculars, while Christian did the same at the other side of the bridge.

'Yes, and the Tommies too, remember,' Hanssen answered. 'Keep your eyes peeled.'

'Like a tomato, sir!' Frensen gave him the traditional answer.

Hanssen grinned and turned to Christian. 'You see, Jungblut, the Tommies have got the exit from the Baltic pretty well sewn up with their Sunderlands and those damned minefields of theirs. We're hoping that by coming through the Canal and edging by Helgoland we're going to fool them. There is simply too much sea around here for them to patrol it. And they don't dare lay mines in case they offend the cheeseheads.' He grinned again. '*Dutch* to you. All right, Ensign Jungblut, you've got that?'

'Yessir.'

'Good. Then the conn is yours. I'm going below.' With that he was clambering down the dripping wet ladder, leaving a surprised Christian in charge for the first time in his life and responsible for the fates of his fellow men. It was a heady - and frightening - feeling.

Two hours later they started to sail by Helgoland, a red smudge in the distance, the weather worsening progressively but still as yet not hindering the good progress the Wolf Pack was making. Somewhere about that time they lost visual contact with the other two U-boats as the rain began to come down in grey sheets. Christian tried his hardest but he couldn't sight them and he was glad when von Arco relieved him. He clambered stiffly down the ladder, stripped naked as they all did when coming off watch in rough seas and staggered to the petty officers' wardroom, where he jack-knifed himself into a bunk which was still warm from its previous occupant's body, pulled up the guard rail to prevent himself from falling out and, wedging himself between closet and wall, tried to sleep.

But it was impossible. The regular *thump-thump* of the diesels, the splashing of the water outside the steel hull and the memory of Paula prevented him from sleeping. After an agony of tossing and turning he drifted off at last.

He woke up in a sweat. '*Juden raus*!' the voice had cried savagely and the fat middle-aged brown-shirt had been advancing on a terrified, naked Paula, his rubber truncheon held in front of his pot belly like a frightening black penis.

The U-69 was rocking wildly. They had left the shelter of the coast now and were receiving the full force of the North Sea. He rubbed his eyes which felt full of coarse sand. It was almost his time to go on watch again. Hurriedly he flung himself into his still damp clothes and pulled on his oilskins, his body feeling infinitely weary. Maydag thrust a steaming mug into his hand. '"Nigger sweat", Ensign.' He winked knowingly. 'Tarted up a little, if yer know what I mean, Ensign.'

Christian took a tentative sip and choked. He knew well what the little man meant. Somehow he had smuggled rum aboard. His 'nigger-sweat' was well laced with it. Christian knew he should report the fact to the Skipper but he didn't. The men trusted and liked him even though he was a budding officer. Somehow he didn't think they'd 'tart up' von Arco's 'nigger sweat'.

Up top the sea had gone crazy. Icy-cold sheets of spray and green water slashed across the bridge. Time and time again the U-69 shuddered as it slammed into the breakers, meeting each one as if it had just run into a brick wall. Everywhere the sea was running hard and wild. Hastily he fastened himself to the bridge with the steel belt and, taking up his big heavy binoculars, started to scan the lowering, threatening sky.

Time passed leadenly as they ploughed relentlessly north-west. The diesels throbbed monotonously. Cascades of water drenched the bridge. The towel which he had wrapped round his neck on the advice of the 'old hares', as the veterans called themselves, was soon soaked. Sea water began to run down his neck and chest. Soon it would be sloshing about inside his seaboots. He felt utterly miserable - and excited!

Now Christian forced himself to ignore the heaving mountains of green water and the icy flying spray and concentrate on the horizon. Today there could be no danger from the 'damned Sunderlands', as the skipper always called the flying boats of the RAF's Coastal Command. But if *they* could sail in such weather, so could the surface ships of the Royal Navy; and the North Sea was dominated by the Tommies.

Suddenly the gloom parted and he saw something. He lifted up his glasses. There was no doubt about it. There was something out there. 'Shadow bearing . . . three zero zero, sir.'

Hanssen, who had the watch, swung his own glasses up and peered in the direction indicated. 'Good work, Jungblut!' he rasped. 'It's a freighter . . . *And it's a Tommy*!'

'Will we attack?' Jungblut began, his nerves already tingling electrically at the prospect of action.

But already the Captain was starting to rap out his orders: '*On battle stations . . . Right full rudder . . . Steer three two zero . . .*'

Abruptly all was controlled excitement as the hands rushed to take up their stations and the U-69 started to turn. Throughout the boat the red alarm lights flooded on, bathing the sweat-glazed faces with a blood-red hue. Now they tensed over their instruments, seemingly not breathing, their eyes bulging out of their heads like madmen.

Von Arco at the attack table called out, 'Lined up!'

Hanssen nodded his approval without taking his binoculars off the freighter and called down, 'Tune into the international radio traffic. I want to know if her Skipper is calling for help.'

'Tubes one to five – ready!' Frensen up in the torpedo compartment reported.

Von Arco relayed the report to the bridge. Christian, standing next to the Skipper, could feel his heart thumping wildly as if it might burst out of his ribcage at any moment. The tension was almost too much. Never before had he experienced such wild excitement. He did not know it, but it was the excitement of the hunter about to kill.

Now, almost as if it sensed it was in danger, the freighter had changed its course. All that was visible of it to the bridge party was its stern. Suddenly their target had become very small.

Hanssen reacted at once. He turned the U-69 into the wind. Immediately the submarine began to pitch and roll violently as the full force of the sea beat against her. Desperately Christian grabbed for support. Hanssen did not seem to notice. He stood there, feet firmly braced, needing no support as he followed the progress of their victim through his glasses, his face set in a wolfish grin. There would be no escaping him, Christian could see that.

Down below, von Arco hurriedly checked his calculations and called up, 'Target red ninety . . . speed sixteen knots . . . seven thousand metres . . . running depth seven metres.'

Christian listened hard, trying to interpret the mass of details. The torpedoes had been set at seven metres' depth so that they would pass under the freighter at about two metres. There the magnetic fire pistols would fire the charges and cause the tin fish to explode. Hopefully they would break the Tommy's back.

'Fire at four thousand!' Hanssen rapped. 'Aim at her foremast!'

'Yessir.'

Now Christian watched entranced as they crept ever closer to their target. He burned with that old primeval fever of the hunter. Now he could no longer feel the icy slap of the waves on his burning face or the water streaming down inside his overalls. Ahead of them lay their first target - nothing else counted. Christian's eyes were narrowed to slits as he followed the progress of their doomed victim. Down below he knew Frensen would be standing by his deadly tin fish, while von Arco kept his finger on the firing push.

Hanssen took the boat down a little so that they seemed to be riding just on top of the water. The force of the sea increased. The waves lashed their crimson faces savagely. The freighter loomed up larger and larger. Even he, veteran that he was, radiated tension, his face hard and set, never taking his eyes off the enemy ship for a moment. The gap between them narrowed and narrowed.

Suddenly the unsuspecting English Skipper played right into their hands. He swung the freighter's bow towards the U-boat. Hanssen threw the U-69 into the attack position. Now she presented the smallest possible target in case the freighter was armed. It would be any moment now. Christian found he was holding his breath, his gloved hands clenched to tight fists. The Skipper would have to fire . . . *he would have to*!

'Fire when ready!' he barked.

'*Ready*!' von Arco snapped.

'*On . . . on . . . on*!' Frensen yelled from where he was crouched over his deadly fish, the back of his singlet black with sweat.

'*FEUER*!' Hanssen yelled.

There was a sudden shudder. A hiss of escaping air. Two torpedoes leapt from the U-69's side as the engineer began to flood automatically to compensate for the change of weight.

As one, the men on the bridge flung up their glasses. For a moment Christian could see the fringe of exploding bubbles as the tin fish sped towards the target.

Abruptly the grey sky was split by a cherry-red flame. A

moment later it was followed by the roar of high explosive. Christian gasped as the blast wave hit him across the face like a flabby fist.

Suddenly the freighter began to break in half as the great yell of triumph ran through the boat: '*A hit . . . a hit . . . Hurrah*!' And at the radio the sweating operator cried urgently, 'They're sending out a message . . . *Sir, they're radioing for help* . . .'

CHAPTER 2

Thoughtfully the First Sea Lord dipped the end of his cigar in his glass of brandy and sucked it, plump baby-face set and worried.

Payne waited. Outside, one of the communist salesmen of the *Daily Worker* was crying, '*Down with this capitalist war! Read what Secretary Pollitt has to say about the real aims of the Government. Down with the capitalist war* . . !' Payne frowned. The nation's spirit was bad. Thank God there were people like the First Sea Lord to put some fire into the nation. Most civilians seemed to think that the war would soon be over without a shot being fired.

Churchill put down the message they had just received from the sinking freighter and said, lisping slightly because he was not wearing his teeth, 'What are we to make of it, eh Payne? First the freighter and then these intercepts from Room Thirty-Nine.* Three Hun submarines conversing with each other. Better bring in this young feller from Room Thirty-Nine. Let us see if he can enlighten us.'

'Yessir.' Payne walked to the door and Churchill observed that he moved as if he had had a hot poker stuffed up his pin-striped arse. 'Lieutenant Fleming,' he called.

A tall, thin-faced officer, with somewhat cruel-looking lips, appeared through the door. Churchill saw that his sleeve was decorated with the curled golden bands of the Royal Naval Reserve. He was a 'wavy-navy' type; probably

* Naval Intelligence

intelligent after all, he concluded.

The man who would one day create James Bond clicked to attention. Churchill waved him to a seat and said, 'Sit down, young fellah, and tell me what you backroom boffins have come up with in Room Thirty-Nine.'

'May I smoke, sir?' Lieutenant Fleming asked, unawed by the presence of the great man.

'Why yes,' Churchill answered, a little surprised. It was very rare that junior officers requested such things in his presence.

Slowly, deliberately, Fleming took out a gold-rimmed cigarette and fitted it into a long black and white cigarette holder while Payne watched amazed. Fleming was the typical old Etonian: everything with style, he told himself. Fleming blew a slow smoke ring and began. 'Well, sir,' he said, drawing at his three-ring Moorland Special, 'the U-boat which sank the freighter obviously belonged to a pack of three – 'Wolf Packs' is what they are called now by the Huns.'

Churchill was impressed. 'In the Old War,' he declared, 'they always hunted alone. Why threes?'

'Dunno sir. New tactic,' Fleming said in his casual Etonian drawl. 'The problem as we see it in Room Thirty-Nine, however, is this.'

'Are you lecturing me, young man?' Churchill asked, half amused, half angered.

'No sir. Just trying to put across the view of my chief, Admiral Godfrey.'

'Well put it across. Do not dither, Fleming.'

'I *never* dither, sir.'

Outside, the communist newspaper-seller was raving, '*Remember it was Churchill who shot at the strikers back in twenty-six* . . . The *real war is between capital and labour, comrades* . . .' Payne frowned and made as if he was going to close the window.

Gravely Churchill shook his head. 'Let us listen to the

voice of the people – courtesy of Uncle Joe Stalin,' he declared. 'We can only learn.'

'Yessir.'

'So what are the Boche up to, sir?' Fleming answered his own question: 'The department's guess is that they are planning a raid somewhere using new tactics – this 'Wolf Pack' idea.'

'A raid – where?' Churchill asked.

'Well, sir, in the First World War they raided our shores on several occasions. Hartlepool, Scarborough . . .'

'Yes, yes, my boy,' Churchill interrupted him with a wave of his fat pale hand. 'Remember I was one of the King's ministers at the time. I recall those events exceedingly well. Their High Sea Fleet dared not sail so they used hit-and-run tactics. A quick raid and then scuttle off back to port. But then they used *surface* ships. Why should U-boats – underwater craft – use the same tactics, eh?'

'Because, sir, we think that Doenitz, the commander of their U-boat arm, is their most aggressive commander. Of all the German naval commanders he is the only one who has iron in his heart – who is prepared to act. The rest just sit on their thumbs and wait to be ordered to act by the Führer.'

Churchill nodded. 'So where are they going to raid us, my boy?'

Fleming thought for a moment. 'Three likely spots, sir. The Humber, Scapa and perhaps Harwich. Our guess is that Doenitz will attack at a place where he is least expected – and all those three harbours are well defended and difficult to enter. Why should our local commanders expect an attack there, especially as that attack will be coming from *beneath* the sea?'

'I take your point,' Churchill said. 'I shall put the Home Fleet on alert of course. But you can't expect our admirals to be able to defend some five hundred miles or so of coastline and at the same time carry out their already heavy sea-going duties.' Churchill paused suddenly, brow creased in a frown.

Payne and Fleming waited. Outside the *Daily Worker* man was crying, '*A million workers still unemployed. Read the truth about the capitalist war industry . . . Million unemployed . . . Barefoot kids in Wales . . .*'

'I think we should try something different.' Churchill broke his silence finally.

'What, sir?' Fleming asked eagerly.

'Catch them when they least expect it. Catch them on the way back.' Churchill's old eyes gleamed suddenly and he stuck out that pugnacious jaw of his. 'Payne.'

'Sir?'

'Send a signal to the officer commanding Fifth Destroyer Flotilla at Harwich. He is to sail immediately with his full force.'

Payne scribbled furiously while the man who would one day create '007' made mental notes of the Old Man in action. Who knows, one day he might need them.

'He is to patrol off the exit to the Baltic – and that of the North-East Sea Canal.'

Payne looked up, surprised. 'But, sir,' he objected, 'the Germans have already sailed. Why do that?'

Churchill grinned and said, 'Yes, but whatever nasty business they are about, my dear Payne, *they will have to come back won't they?*'

Christian's sense of triumph at their 'kill' vanished immediately. As the U-69 began to move slowly through the thick oil swell filled with debris and wreckage, he could see dead and dying men everywhere.

Men coughing their last, their lungs flooded with diesel oil; men just lying there listlessly letting the sea have its way with them; men screaming with the intolerable pain of their burns, threshing and splashing the water as if in fury;

men floating, stiffening already like pieces of abandoned flotsam.

Hanssen watched the transformation on the young Ensign's face gravely, knowing what might well be going through his mind at this moment, trying to ignore the pleas for aid from the sailors floundering in the water. He could not take them aboard and he could not help them. Soon, if they were lucky, their own craft would appear and pick them up - he hoped.

Solemnly he put his hand on Christian's shoulder. 'Jungblut, this is the face of war. There is nothing glamorous about it, is there?' He indicated the dead man trailing what looked like a purple-green snake behind him in the water; they were his intestines.

Christian shook his head and said, 'No sir.'

'Then remember this always when you have your own boat. This is what our tin fish do, Jungblut. Those men out there, dead or dying, are someone's sons, brothers, fathers. Enemies they might be, but they are also men - human beings like ourselves. Remember that, Jungblut.'

'I will, sir,' Christian replied numbly.

'Good,' Hanssen dismissed him, raising his voice. 'Now get below. We're going to dive before those damned Sunderlands come racing up to drop square eggs on us.' He waited till the bridge watch had clambered down the dripping ladder, then slowly and solemnly he raised his hand to his battered old white cap as if in salute . . .

Hanssen waited as von Arco made up the Deck Log: '*Zero eight hundred hours. Overcast and cloudy with light rain. Wind force five (stiff breeze). Depth trimmed ten metres.*'

He nodded as the second-in-command presented it to him, and signed it while the other officers waited expectantly. This was the moment. They were two days out from Kiel. The time had come for Lt. Commander

Hanssen to open his sealed orders. Hanssen took his time as he broke the red seals and pulled the printed sheet from the envelope. He squinted in the poor green light and began to read: 'At zero ten hundred hours tomorrow morning, gentlemen, we become operational. Exactly twelve hours later at twenty-two hundred hours, *Oberleutnant zur See* Prien in the U-47 will begin execution of the attack plan. His target is . . .' Hanssen hesitated only a moment remembering that shameful day so long ago when he had been young '. . . *Scapa Flow*!'

Someone gasped, and listening at the hatchway Frensen blessed himself and whispered, 'Holy strawsack, kiss me muvver for I'm gonna be the Queen of the Frigging May!'

Next to him Maydag swallowed hard and whispered out of the side of his mouth, 'The whole shitting Tommy battlefleet is located there!'

Hanssen did not seem to notice the sensation that his bald announcement had made; for he continued in an even voice, as if he was talking about the state of the weather. 'Captain Prien will carry out the main attack himself,' he continued, eyes skipping along the lines trying to find the role assigned to the U-69. '*Oberleutnant* Kretschmar of the U-23 will take up a patrol line in the North Sea, away from the Orkneys, in order to prevent any English intervention in the operation.'

'And the U-69, sir?' von Arco asked, heart racing, no longer able to contain himself.

Hanssen looked at him and von Arco lowered his gaze. Could the Skipper feel his fear? Had he seen through him?

'We, Number One?' He looked at the orders once more. 'We are scheduled to be tail-end Charleys?'

'*Tail-end Charleys*?' von Arco echoed, puzzled.

'Yes, according to our orders we are to remain behind when Prien's U-47 has carried out its mission and wait for the rest of the Tommies to emerge.' He smiled coldly. 'Those are Commodore Doenitz' orders.'

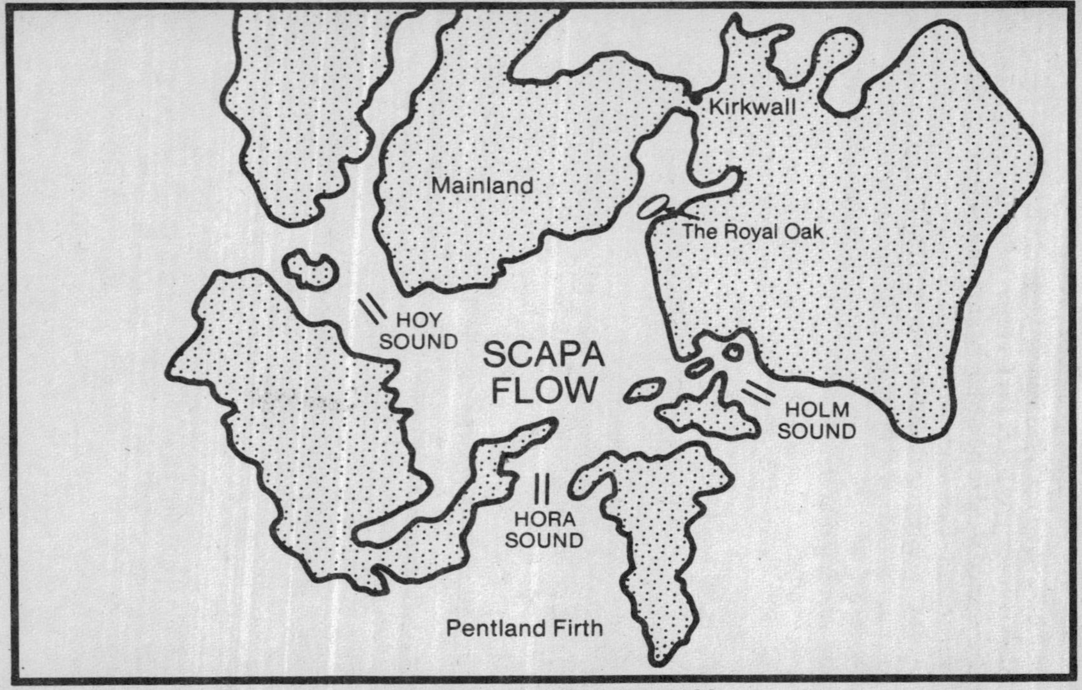

SCAPA FLOW October 1939

'But, sir,' von Arco protested. 'After Prien's attack the balloon will go up. The whole weight of the British Home Fleet will descend upon any German vessel in the vicinity. One doesn't need to be a clairvoyant to know that . . . Why sir,' he said, face ashen, '*it'll be plain suicide*!'

'Yes,' Hansen said calmly. 'Something like that . . .'

CHAPTER 3

HMS *Royal Oak* – all twenty-six thousand tons of her – was a smart ship. Some thought her the smartest in the whole of the Royal Navy. She had been commissioned in style on 7th June 1939, her crew marching out of the Royal Naval Barracks at Portsmouth behind a band, wheeling to the right down Queen Street, on to the Hard and in through the dockyard's main gates to where the *Royal Oak* lay alongside the Southern Railway Jetty.

Over twelve hundred men had boarded her that day, mostly from 'Pompey' and Devonport (where the battle-ship had first been built in World War One). That had been four and a half months before, and the regulars who had boarded her thought they were heading for a two and a half years' cruise in the Mediterranean. Instead the war had sent the ship north to the bleak islands of Orkney where the first ship they had encountered as they entered the anchorage at Scapa had been *Saint Abba*, glittering with white paint and adorned with large red crosses. The sailors of the *Royal Oak* had joked at the sight of the hospital ship: 'Now we know there's going to be a war. The Admiralty are taking care of everything!'

For a while the *Royal Oak* had sailed with the rest of the Home Fleet searching for German surface craft. The weather had been terrible with the slow *Royal Oak* wallowing through the Arctic storms way behind the rest of the fleet like an ancient steel whale. Alone without escort, rattling at every plate, she barely made twelve knots an hour. In the end it was decided she would remain at home in Scapa Flow. The Home Fleet would be dispersed in the face of the mysterious German threat; *the Royal Oak* would remain where it was: a floating anti-aircraft battery manned by twelve hundred regulars.

It was a boring but relaxing duty, positioned as the old battleship was off the bare purple and brown hills, the anchorage empty now save for a few drifters acting as fleet auxiliaries, the hospital ship and the hulk of the German battle-cruiser the *Doerfflinger*, floating bottom up, a permanent reminder that here in 1918 the Imperial German fleet had surrendered to the Royal Navy and then scuttled itself in a last show of beaten pride.

Now, as evening on Friday 13th October 1939 approached, with the long shadows creeping over the still green water of the anchorage, most of the officers and men of the *Royal Oak* were looking forward to a full night off watch and in harbour. Some of them even hoped to be able to snatch a few hours on shore; not that there was much to do there save drink and 'count the frigging sheep', as they joked. Others promised themselves they'd 'go to school' tonight; to one of the many gambling schools – Pontoon Crown, Anchor and the like – which always ran in the gaming space commonly known as 'Monte Carlo' whenever the men were off-duty.

But a few of those hard-bitten regulars were apprehensive, especially the 120 Boys aged between fourteen and seventeen. Somehow a rumour had started among them that the anchorage was going to be bombed by the Germans: 'Friday . . . and the thirteenth as well. *Blooming heck, something's got to happen tonight, lads*!' they said to each other as they squatted in their hammocks in the yellow light. Not even the fact that the BBC's nine o'clock news had announced that this thirteenth had been very unlucky for the Germans – two of their U-boats had been sunk in the Atlantic – could soothe their fears as slowly the great ship began to settle down for the night. 'Friday the thirteenth,' the boys repeated to one another solemnly, 'it ain't right . . . It's a bad omen, I tell yer.'

They were right. Soon they would sleep - before dying violently. All of them . . .

Cautiously Prien raised the periscope. All was dark as it broke the surface. Before him lay two openings into the Flow, clearly outlined against the dark mass of rock. 'Kirk Sound and . . . Skerry sound on the port bow,' he announced.

It was an eerie sight. On land everything was black but high in the sky the Northern Lights flickered so that the bay below was lit a strange, glowing hue. To either side lay the block-ships like the wings of a ghostly theatre. He was not an imaginative man but he told himself that the whole scene made him think of the beginning of a violent, tragic play scene. The stage was set. The drama could commence.

'All right,' he decided, 'here we go. Kirk Sound it is.'

Slowly the 500-ton submarine started to move into the Sound, crawling its way forward metre by metre, a sitting duck now if it was discovered. Everyone sensed it. The faces of the young crewmen were strained and ashen. Here and there some of their cheeks had begun to tick nervously. Their fear was tangible. Prien wiped the sweat from his own brow while the navigation officer held the ship as she began to drift broadsides, carried by the strong current. Twice Prien caught himself just in time, before letting loose angrily at the anxious young officer, his shirt black with sweat. He knew he had to keep a tight rein on the crew - and his own temper. It was vital.

'Block-ship!' he announced. 'To port! *Quick, man!*'

The harassed young officer caught the U-47 just in time and the boat swept by the silent, blacked-out block-ship by a matter of metres. Prien swallowed hard. That had been a close shave.

'*Sound band . . port-ahead*!' the rating cried.

Prien dashed to the periscope at once, his nerves tingling electrically, but making no noise, for like the rest of the crew in accordance with the 'silent running rules' he had slipped a pair of socks over his shoes.

'Up scope,' he commanded. 'Right so!' he bent down, almost on his knees, and peered through the instrument. It had broken the surface of the Sound. 'Down scope . . . too much. Up . . . up . . . up,' he ordered, his heart thumping like a trip-hammer. Now it was barely above the fringe of the waves. Hastily he swung his white cap round, brim to the rear, and looked at the scene.

A black shape leapt into view, a mass of white water churning at its stern. It was some sort of coastal vessel - perhaps a supply ship - and it was obvious its Skipper did not know he was being trailed in by an enemy submarine.

He breathed a heartfelt sigh of relief. 'It's all right. Another craft ahead of us. Hasn't spotted us.'

One of the ratings laughed crazily and Prien shot him a hard look. The laughter froze on his young, haggard face. The crew were nearing the end of their tethers. It was time they got through.

The minutes passed leadenly while Prien remained glued to the periscope watching the bank swing alarmingly into view more than once as the race increased in speed and the navigation officer fought desperately to keep the submarine on course. 'Heaven, arse and cloudburst,' he cursed to himself. If they got stuck on one of those banks he'd spend the rest of the damned war behind barbed wire . . . and that would be an end to the 'tin'.

But *Oberleutnant zur See* Prien need not have worried. He'd earn a whole drawerful of 'tin' before fate overtook him. He would never see an Allied cage, neither during the War nor after it. For by then he would have long vanished . . .

*

On the *Royal Oak* it was ten-thirty as the last record was placed on the ship's broadcasting system. As usual it was 'Goodnight My Love'. Now the Marines started going around the great ship checking that the ratings had turned in and that all seadoors were closed.

The 'Guest Night' which had been going on in the officers' gunroom began to break up. Most of the junior officers had to be on duty early next morning, for the *Royal Oak* was due to shift to another berth at seven o'clock. A few officers lingered, throwing dice. A Marine officer drew nine Jacks and one Queen in a straight throw. 'Now who's Friday the thirteenth unlucky for, eh gentlemen?' he chortled. He took out a cigarette and lit it. Matches were short and two other officers asked for a light for their cigarettes from the same match. 'Not scared of being number three?' the Marine asked.

'Hell no! Besides, in an hour's time Friday the thirteenth 1939 will be dead,' the third officer said, taking the match easily. *Soon he would be too.*

'*Midnight*, gentlemen . . . comrades,' Prien announced, taking his aching eyes away from the periscope for a moment, 'and we're in. We've done it! We're through the Sound . . . *Scapa Flow is ours*!'

The crew's haggard faces lit up. If it had not been for the silent running regulations Prien knew they would have cheered out loud. They had achieved what had been thought impossible: they had penetrated Great Britain's mightiest naval harbour undetected. 'So now all we have to do is find the plumpest pigeons, comrades,' he continued, 'and proceed to sink them.'

'Gobble them up, sir - pigeons, sir,' his second-in-command corrected him.

'Yes, of course.' Prien was businesslike again. 'Radio operator, signal the captains of the U-23 and U-69 that we are here.' Prien thought for a fleeting moment of how envious the other two skippers would be when they received his message. Hard luck on them. This was going to be Prien's triumph - and he deserved it. 'Signal, too, that I am expecting to attack - in about thirty minutes time. All right - up periscope!' There was the usual soft hiss of compressed air escaping and the periscope broke the surface. Hastily Prien pressed his eyes to it and gasped. Less than three thousand metres away, clearly outlined a stark black in the gleaming circle of calibrated glass, there was a huge ship. 'A big fellow,' he breathed. 'We've got a big one - right in front of us!' He swallowed hard and tried to contain his mounting excitement. 'Action stations everyone. We're going to take out the big fellow!'

His Majesty's Ship the *Royal Oak* now had exactly one hour left.

CHAPTER 4

At one o'clock on the morning of Saturday 14th October an explosion forrad shook the sleeping *Royal Oak*. It was followed immediately by a thundering, cascading rattle and clatter. The anchor cables were running out, out of control. Suddenly the ship was filled with the smell of burning paint and acrid smoke.

Abruptly the ship's tannoys blared into crackling, metallic life. A calm, upper-class voice announced, 'We've been hit forrad . . . probably by an aerial bomb . . . We've been hit –'

The announcement was drowned by a second explosion. The great ship – nearly thirty thousand tons of her – swayed and shook as if in the grip of some gigantic fist.

'Don't worry, it's Saturday the fourteenth!' someone cried and then he too was running down the deck for his life, as everywhere the men not on duty started to tumble from their hammocks and grab for their uniforms, the ship's sirens and whistles already shrilling their dread warning.

Immediately all was controlled but frantic activity. Officers and men were doubling back and forth everywhere in the crowded gangways as a thick, choking, black fog started to sweep through the stricken ship, which was already beginning to list noticeably. Now water was rushing in the great holes ripped beneath her water line and she began to shake and judder, altering her trim from moment to moment so that the men attempting to escape felt like alpinists ascending a shuddering steel mountain.

The open ventilators on her starboard side touched the sea. Immediately tons of water began to pour into the *Royal Oak*. Below decks the lights went out abruptly. Now there was nothing to see by except the glow of the many fires which had broken out. Men screamed with fear. They panicked, grasping and thrusting at their shipmates in terror as they fought their way through the ankle-deep water in an attempt to escape. 'Remember you're British, lads,' older petty officers yelled desperately. 'Don't panic . . . *For fuck's sake don't panic*!'

Now the ship was heeling slowly and remorselessly to starboard. Men fought to reach the doors through the milling, shouting, cursing mob, packing the inky darkness of the littered decks. But the doors wouldn't open at that angle. Shrieking obscenely, they tore off their fingernails, their hands running with blood as they clawed at the unyielding steel. Some found a steel ladder leading to the upper deck. An old man, false teeth bulging out of a wizened yellow face, lit match after match to guide them upwards, saying gently, 'Take it easy, lads . . . Take it easy.'

The men fighting frantically, clinging to the rungs with all their strength, kicking off those who in their unreasoning terror tried to pull them off, battled their way upwards. Behind them the old man with matches still kept calling, 'Take it easy, lads . . . take it . . .'

The ship had heeled over to an angle of forty-five degrees now. Soon it would turn completely. Those still on board would be taken down with it to the bottom of the sea and trapped alive. Now she was racked by a series of explosions as the boilers went up. Terrible screams came floating up from below as the scalded stokers fought to escape. But there was no escape for any of the poor wretches still on the *Royal Oak*.

Now even the deck coverings on the upper deck were on fire. Smoke - thick, oily and inky black - was pouring out from holes ripped into the ship's plating. Men preparing to dive overboard lost their footing and rolled helplessly into these flaming furnaces, vanishing for ever, trailing hysterically drawn-out screams behind them. Everywhere there was the gurgling of water as it poured in relentlessly. It would not be very long now.

Startlingly the *Royal Oak* gave another great lurch as bulkheads gave way on all sides. Like a massive steel whale she rolled right over. Those still on the burning deck were flung into the water covered in escaped oil or were carried right beneath the wreck. There was a tremendous noise like a huge tin filled with loose nails being rattled furiously. Suddenly her port propellor shaft reared high up out of the water so that the swimming men could see it standing stark black against the ruddy light like a great crucifix - and then she went under. With her she carried eight hundred men, dead and alive. Huge bubbles of trapped air started to explode on the surface. The sea boiled. A great wave spread outwards and then slowly the water calmed again around the handful of survivors. *Oberleutnant zur See* Prien had sunk the *Royal Oak* at last.

Prien solemnly touched his hand to his cap in salute as the warship slid beneath the waves in the circle of calibrated glass and his crew cheered wildly at their victory, the silent running regulations thrown to the winds. Then he was businesslike again. Now the balloon would certainly go up. Already he could see the searchlights on shore flicking on, one by one, in sudden alarm. They'd start hunting him soon. 'Radio operator,' he barked as the periscope started hissing down, 'signal our success to the captains of the U-23 and U-69.'

The radio operator, his face still bruised where Frensen had hit him with those cruel brass knuckles, grinned maliciously. 'Yes sir,' he chortled. 'I'll tell those lickers of the *Sixty-Nine*!'

'We'll be coming out of the Flow at' – Prien made a quick calculation – 'approximately zero six thirty hours. Just before first light. Let them prepare.' He swung round on the second-in-command. 'All right, that's it.'

'But we've still got five torpedoes left, sir,' the Number One objected. 'And there must be other ships in the anchorage. If –'

'No ifs,' Prien interrupted him in that harsh, unreasoning manner of his. He had achieved his 'kill'; he was not going to risk his neck any longer. He had made his decision on that score hours ago. 'We're returning to base.'

'Yes sir!' the other officer snapped and hurried to the controls to carry out his duties. To leave the Flow after torpedoing one ship and with the anchorage still asleep was hardly heroic. But he knew his Skipper. He would tolerate no objections.

Slowly the submarine began to enter the Sound once more. Behind her, the rescue boats started to swarm out to rescue the handful of burnt, broken men swimming in the freezing water . . .

Von Arco flushed angrily. 'Prien is obviously very full of himself, sir,' he snapped handing back the message from the U-47 to Hanssen.

The Skipper shrugged. 'He has every right to be, von Arco. Never mind, *Oberleutnant*, there'll be plenty of action now – for everybody. All right, up periscope!' He waited till it slid up the tube and then, turning his battered white cap, he peered through the scope.

Dawn had already broken. A dirty white light was flushing the horizon, a brown smudge beyond the heaving grey sea. Carefully he searched the circle of the horizon, taking his time, knowing that the pursuit of Prien's boat must have started by now.

'Faint beat of ship's engine,' the operator at the hydrophone sang out. 'Can't identify.'

'Thank you, *Obermaat* . . .' Hanssen stopped suddenly. Hastily he adjusted the fine controls. Yes, there it was, stark black against the green translucent wash of the sea. A ship – an enemy ship. There was no mistaking that white bone in her teeth. It was a Tommy destroyer looking for Prien's craft. Hanssen made up his mind; he would attack. 'Clear all torpedo-tubes,' he commanded.

Hastily Frensen and the other torpedo-operators drove out the sea water from their tubes and thrust home their deadly fish.

Hanssen took a fix on the enemy destroyer which was getting larger by the minute. Behind it he could see the spouts of water hurtling upwards. Obviously the enemy ship was dropping a pattern of depth charges. Prien could well be in trouble. He had to help him.

'Bearing red seven zero . . . I am twenty degrees starboard,' he rasped out the commands. 'Port wheel five knots . . . steer three hundred and fifty degrees . . . *DOWN PERISCOPE!*'

Now they worried themselves sick in the control room as the boat began to turn slowly to its new course. Had they estimated the enemy's course correctly? How long was the U-69 going to take turning? Where would the Tommy destroyer be when they upped the periscope once more?

Standing close to Hanssen, Christian could almost feel him thinking hard, his brain racing, as he worried about what would happen in the next few moments. He found himself breathing hard as if he were running a race, his fists clenched and damp with sweat.

Impatiently Hanssen watched for the torpedo-tube

lights to flick on. Time was running out fast. 'When the hell are Numbers Two and Three going to be ready, von Arco?' he snapped in the same instant that the lights flashed.

Now the electric motors whined ever louder. They were driving forward relentlessly towards the enemy. Christian started to count off the minutes before the skipper would order the boat's periscope up. Behind him the hydrophone operator called out at regular intervals, voice thick with suppressed tension, 'Engine noise getting louder sir . . . getting . . . louder . . .'

Christian could feel the tension in the air. The excitement was almost unbearable.

'Up periscope!' Hanssen's command made him jump with shock. He bent immediately and started to call out his orders: 'Bearing green twenty-five degrees.'

The answer came promptly 'You are now twenty-five degrees starboard, sir.'

'He's more than that!' Hanssen snapped. 'Give him forty-five degrees.'

'Enemy's new course zero forty degrees,' the reply came singing back.

Hanssen straightened up. 'Down periscope. Starboard wheel. Nine knots. Steer three hundred and ten degrees. Down ten metres.'

Christian felt the sweat dripping from him. His face flushed and his heart began to pound frantically. Something had to give soon; this strain was just too much.

'*Up periscope*!' Hanssen ordered again. This was it. 'Stand by!' he cried after a moment. He pressed the button of his stop-watch and counted off the seconds: '*One . . . two . . . three . . .*'

Christian held his breath.

'*FIRE*!' The boat shuddered violently. 'Down periscope!' Hanssen bellowed urgently . . . 'Down to twenty metres!'

They waited in dead silence, hardly daring to breathe. Like the rest of the crew Christian had his gaze fixed almost hypnotically on the control room clock. It seemed to creep round the dial as they waited to hear whether their fish had struck.

One minute . . . two minutes . . . two minutes and thirty seconds . . . Christian's doubts and uncertainties grew agonizingly. *They'd missed*! He strained his ears for any sound. But all he heard was the hum and *tick-tick* of the helmsman's gyro and the faint noises of the sea outside their steel hull. *Three minutes.* It was now or never.

Nothing!

Christian gave up hope. Hanssen, as tense and as haggard as the rest, mopped his brow. 'We must have –'

Suddenly there was a muffled bang and he stopped short, eyes wild with excitement: The lights flickered off and on. Another bang . . . and another. A gentle tremor shook the deck plates. Christian looked at the sweating Skipper in disbelief. Hanssen swallowed hard and said huskily, 'Take her up to periscope depth, Number One.'

A moment later the officers were taking turns to stare through the periscope. Christian, the ensign, was last and in a flash the whole terrific picture leapt into his view in all its terrible drama.

To left and right exploding ammunition arched outwards through the black smoke to whirl like giant fireballs. Beneath, her back broken, the English destroyer was sinking fast, men throwing themselves overboard or scrambling down the steep sides to drop the last few metres into the heaving water, peppered everywhere by falling debris. 'She's going,' Hanssen said at his side. 'A terrible thing . . . a dying ship. Now Jungblut away from –'

Like the hammer of doom the first depth charge exploded right above the U-69, sending her reeling through the water, the crew deafened and stunned by this surprise attack. As the lights went out and the first panicked cries of fear and rage could be heard, Hanssen knew that they were going to pay for Prien's success. *The English were on to them*!

CHAPTER 5

'Report damage,' Hanssen whispered before the U-69 suddenly reeled, as another burst of depth charges exploded all about them with a shattering roar. Once more the U-boat shuddered and trembled. Somewhere a valve blew. A fountain of water arced through the aisle. Christian tumbled backwards under the blast completely soaked.

From all sides the reports came flooding in. It was now an hour since they had been surprised and the race of screws above them was everywhere, easily audible to them all.

Another salvo exploded savagely. It just missed the conning-tower. The U-69 was driven even deeper into the depths. Just in time Hein levelled her off before she rammed the bottom. This brought down a new series of depth charges. They could even hear them splashing into the water. The Tommies knew they were there and they were determined to make up for the loss of the *Royal Oak* and the deaths of those eight hundred sailors.

Now their pursuers stepped up the attack. The haggard submariners could hear the *ping-ping* of the Asdic, the threshing screws which came and went, grew nearer, stopped, ground into reverse and came back once more; each time they brought with them imminent death in the form of those terrible canisters filled with high explosive.

Then their hearts seemed to stop beating as the sparks flew and the bombs hammered against their tin coffin, punching the U-69 from side to side as if it were a toy, leaving them gasping with shock, eyes bulging in terror, their breath coming in harsh gulps, as if they could not force enough air into their lungs.

'*Sharks and little fishes*,' Christian told himself. But now the Tommies were the sharks and all of them from the Skipper to the most junior rating were the little fishes! Would it never damnwell end?

Suddenly - surprisingly at this moment of acute danger - he found himself thinking of the Jewish girl he had loved: Paula Petersen. He was like her now; fighting for survival with everyman's hand against her. But he had comrades. He wasn't alone. His heart went out to her in far-off Hamburg. Somehow, if he ever got out of this trap, he would help her, see that she left Germany, had a chance to make a fresh start in a new country. At that moment, at the height of the deadly attack, with the U-69 reeling from blow after blow, Christian Jungblut swore to himself that he would help Paula.

A second later another salvo of bombs exploded all around them. The emergency lights went out. Christian hung on grimly. Switching on the flashlight pinned to his breast, he was horrified to see the needle of the depth gauge swinging wildly, while the two planesmen hung on to their wheels in absolute confusion. They were going down rapidly.

Again Hanssen rallied the terrified men while von Arco crouched with his back to the bulkhead of the control room, face glazed with sweat, eyes bulging and wild with fear - completely useless. Somehow or other he managed to level the boat off, halting that tremendous dive to destruction until she stopped, the depth gauge reading an amazing 260 metres below the surface. 'By rights,' he gasped, mopping his streaming brow as the emergency lighting flickered on once more, 'the hull should have been crushed five minutes ago.' He forced a weary grin.

'But perhaps the old gent sitting up there on a cloud feels a little for his poor submariners after all.'

'Take more than a frigging tin-opener to open the U-69 sir!' Frensen called loyally from the bow.

'Well said, Frensen. Now knock it off all of you. Silent running and let's conserve air.'

The hours passed. But still the English did not relax the pressure. As dusk descended the wind above let up and the sea calmed. As a result the enemy depth charge attack increased in ferocity. Even at that depth the exploding canisters made the water roar and rumble furiously, buffeting the U-69 from side to side as if she were a child's toy.

Christian became conscious of the gradual tightening of his chest muscles. He reacted angrily. His body was trying to take over even though he had his mind under control. He forced himself to relax and slow down his rate of breathing which had increased and was becoming hectic. At the same time he forced himself too to forget about breathing. For he knew if he didn't, he would start breathing fast again and begin to suffer a kind of slow suffocation. That would make him dizzy and his brain would start to race. Panic would set in. But he knew that though he had himself under control, there were those among the crew who had almost reached the end of their tether, as that damned bombardment went on and on.

Most of the crew lolled around like wilting flowers. Their eyes bulged and their mouths sagged open stupidly. But they had their breathing under control and no fear showed in their faces. But there were others who shivered and trembled as if they were in the throes of some terrible tropical fever, occasionally muttering frantically to themselves.

Christian could see that von Arco belonged to this group. He had given up any attempt to conceal his fears. He slumped opposite, his face a twitching, eerie green, his hands moving constantly, a nerve ticking regularly at the side of his shaven head. Christian knew that the Skipper had noticed von Arco's collapse too. But for reasons known only to himself, he did not say anything. Perhaps, Christian told himself, Hanssen reasoned that any criticism levelled at an officer might set off a panic among the weaker members of the crew.

By eight o'clock that night they knew a decision had to be made. There was no more leeway left. Their air was running out rapidly. It was either suicide or surrender. 'Hein,' he commanded, 'let's release some compressed air. Might give us another hour before . . .' He left the rest of his sentence unsaid, but they all knew what he meant.

'Yessir,' Hein said. Choking and gasping with the lack of air, his movements feeble and clumsy as if his hands were clothed in boxing-gloves, he carried out the Skipper's orders. He released some compressed air from the midship buoyancy tank. Slowly the U-69 began to rise.

The enemy reacted immediately. A salvo of depth charges rained down upon them. The U-69 rocked violently. She was going straight up to the surface. 'Alarm stations!' Hanssen yelled frantically. 'We're going to the top!'

Next moment, however, another salvo slammed into the U-69 with savage fury and she started to sink once more, the men crawling on their hands and knees in the dim green light to distribute the weight before she slapped into the bottom bow-first. Finally, at the very last moment, the battered, scarred boat levelled out and at a record three hundred metres vibrated to a stop, after a series of convulsive, terrifying shakes.

Hanssen wiped his dripping brow and said, 'Well done, Hein, I thought we were all going to go hop that time. All right, comrades, on with masks.'

Wearily the crewmen fumbled for the mouthpieces of the rubber hoses attached to their masks, drawing in hot, purified air through potash cartridges. Almost immediately they started to cough and choke. The temperature rose at once. Coughing and sweating now, they waited again.

Five minutes later they lurched under a single, shattering blow. It sounded like a gigantic club thrashing a sheet of tinplate. Some men nearly fell from their perches. Opposite Christian, von Arco's eyes bulged from his head in sheer, naked, unreasoning fear. Hastily Hanssen grabbed him by the hand and pressed hard, digging his fingers into von Arco's flesh cruelly, willing him not to rip off his mask. Von Arco calmed down as blue smoke started to drift into the littered, waterlogged interior of the trapped submarine.

'Few bangs won't hurt anyone,' Hanssen said, taking out his rubber tube. 'Perhaps the Tommy bastards are going to leave us in peace now. Perhaps they're telling themselves at this very moment that we've all bitten into the grass for good.' He smiled encouragingly but wearily and stuck the tube back into his mouth. He started to cough once more.

Now the only sound was their coughing and gasping and the squeaking and groaning of the hull as every centimetre of the metal skin was subjected to an immense pressure: two hundred tons to every square metre, - and the plating was a mere two centimetres thick! It was an awesome thought and Christian didn't dwell on it. Instead he started to count off the minutes since that last gigantic salvo, gaze fixed on the clock as if mesmerized.

Hanssen caught his look and nodded encouragingly, a smile in his tired eyes, fingers pressed together in the German sign for good luck.

Five minutes ticked by . . . *ten* . . . *fifteen* . . . In spite of their plight, some of them began to hope. The Tommies might have gone after all . . . *Twenty* . . . By sheer willpower, Hanssen forced himself not to move . . . *Twenty-five minutes* . . . His eyes sought and found the spanner he would use . . . *Thirty long minutes – One whole half hour had passed without another depth charge attack*!

He took the tube out of his mouth and staggered over to where the big spanner lay in the ankle-deep water. Watched intently by those who were still conscious, he laboured to the hull, then raised the spanner slowly - very slowly - as if it weighed a ton, and struck the hull. There was a great hollow boom. Hanssen sank to his knees like a boxer trying to fight off a count of ten.

Christian tensed, waiting with bated breath. His nerves tingled, as if they were naked, exposed to a dentist's drill.

The minutes passed by with Hanssen still on his knees, gasping for breath, chest heaving as if he was running a great race. He took off his treasured white cap. His hair was damp and matted with sweat. Exhausted as he was, Christian was still shocked that it had begun to turn white. He was an old man.

FIVE MINUTES . . . TEN MINUTES . . . The men were slumping down everywhere, drifting off into unconsciousness - and death . . . *FIFTEEN MINUTES* . . . And there had been no response to the hammer blow. *THE TOMMIES HAD GIVEN UP AT LAST*!

Wearily Hanssen rose to his feet, swaying groggily. He drew a deep breath, almost a sigh of resignation, as if he could not trust himself to speak. 'All right,' he croaked, 'take her up . . . They've gone.'

CHAPTER 6

'Open ventilators - clean the boat!' Hanssen cried, sucking in great drafts of icy sea air, as a weary cheer went up from down below. 'Look-outs to your posts . . . Von Arco you take over -'

The rest of his words were drowned by a thunderous explosion. A blinding blue flame shot the length of the dripping deck like the searing arc of a blow-torch. Below, controls shattered. Glass splinters whizzed through the air. A gyro compass slammed against a bulkhead like a shell.

'*Captain*!' Christian cried as he clambered up the dripping ladder.

Hanssen screamed as a piece of flying shrapnel from the second shell hit him full force in the face and he slammed against the side of the conning-tower. 'Get out of my way!' he choked as Christian tried to grab him. He blundered forward. Something seemed to be impeding his vision. He tried to raise his right arm to remove the sudden darkness. Nothing happened. *He had no right arm*! It had been severed at the elbow. Now bright-scarlet blood jetted from the gory stump. He fell back against the steel wall once more. 'Where are you, Jungblut? In three devils' name, man, point me in the right direction!'

'Captain, sir,' Christian pleaded, 'you've been badly hit.' He wrapped his hands around the arm above the stump and pressed hard.

Angrily Hanssen shrugged him off and pulled himself upright again. 'Leave me alone. What is it that fired at us just then?' he demanded.

Christian stared across the heaving waves, an icy green in the spectral light of the sickle moon. 'Small craft, sir, to port. A trawler or something of that nature . . .' He ducked automatically as another shell struck the water a few metres away. A huge spout of sea water shot into the air and came cascading down to drench the little group of men on the bridge.

'Sounds like a Tommy seventy-five millimetre to me!' Hanssen cried above the roar. 'Have we a chance to submerge, Jungblut?'

'She's coming straight at us full lick, sir.' He could see the sudden surge of wild white water at the enemy vessel's bow.

'Good, get the gun crew up top - at the double! Von Arco, where in God's name are you? Stand by with the torpedoes. *Los, los, wirds bald?*'

As the crew were galvanized into electric action, Christian, standing by to catch Hanssen, gasped in wonder. The Skipper was blinded, his face dripping down onto his chest like molten red wax, and he was dying on his feet; yet he was absolutely, totally in command.

Von Arco clattered up to the bridge. He recoiled with horror at the sight of that horrendous red mask and the twin pits where the eyes had once been.

'Von Arco, take over,' Hanssen commanded. 'I have been hit. I am afraid I can't see.' He sagged suddenly and Christian caught him just before he fell. 'Von Arco, don't you hear me, man?'

Von Arco remained standing there, frozen into petrified immobility, as if for all time, as he took in that terrible scene: the shattered bridge, the dying captain, with beyond the enemy vessel racing towards them at top speed for the kill.

'Report!' Hanssen yelled with the last of his strength. 'Report, damn you!'

'I can't . . .' von Arco choked, twisting his head to one side as if he was being strangled.

Hanssen was dying and he couldn't see; but his mind was still active enough to know that von Arco had broken down completely at last. 'Take over the torpedoes, Ensign Jungblut. I shall guide you. Hurry, man! They'll be on us in a moment!'

Again the U-69 reeled alarmingly as a shell struck her aft. Rigging came tumbling down. The radio mast hit the water, crackling madly, little blue sparks running its length. At the 88mm gun one of the crew flung up his arms as if he was climbing the rungs of an invisible ladder, fighting to remain upright, before he fell backwards into the heaving water screaming hysterically.

Von Arco started to sob.

Still supporting the dying Skipper, Christian, suddenly icy cool and in complete command of himself, started to rap out his orders, prompted by Hanssen: 'Stand by for surface fire.'

'Tubes One, Three and Five,' Hanssen gasped.

'Tubes One, Three and Five ready, sir,' Frensen acknowledged from below.

'The range, Jungblut!'

Christian rapped it out as yet another shell slammed into the U-69 and the 88mm seemed to disintegrate, its long barrel dropping as its crew fell dead across it. Hanssen shuddered. He was failing fast now. 'Carry on, Ensign Jungblut,' he quavered.

Christian did not hesitate '*FIRE*!' he yelled.

There was a hiss. The U-69 lurched. Another hiss as a second torpedo spurted from the submarine. The two deadly fish raced towards the enemy craft, trailing a wake of boiling white water behind them.

Desperately the Skipper of the English boat attempted

to throw his craft round, out of the torpedo's way. The first one hissed by his bow harmlessly, missing the vessel by metres. But the second struck home. There was a spurt of angry, cherry-red flame. The sound of rending metal. Suddenly the English ship came to a halt, as if it had just run into a brick wall, one of its masts showering down right across the bridge.

'You've hit her, Jungblut! You've hit . . .' He stopped suddenly. Christian's cry of joy died on his lips. He turned and gasped. Lt. Commander Hanssen hung there on his arm - *dead.*

Dawn came reluctantly, as if God almost refused to throw his light on this cold, grey, war-torn world. Behind them the English vessel still burned on the horizon, sending up a huge column of oily black smoke; occasionally, a star shell would explode above it, turning the sea an icy silver. Soon they would be spotted by a prowling Sunderland and then, Christian knew as he stood there on the bridge, there would be all hell to pay. Before then he had to escape.

But the U-69 seemed unable to raise power. While Hein worked desperately on the damaged engines below, he had to ensure that the battered ship kept pushing on, though at a painfully slow speed, trailing bits and pieces of its shattered superstructure behind it in the water.

Next to him Frensen, manning the twin 20mm flak cannon, wiped the dewdrop from the end of his crimson nose and declared, 'Good skipper we've lost in Commander Hanssen. One of the old school. The crew liked him a lot!'

'The officers too,' Christian said, not taking his eyes off the grey, lowering sky for an instant, his mind still on the blinded, bullet-riddled Skipper now lying dead in his own little cabin, sightless eyes staring at the picture of his wife and children whom he would never see again.

'Not all of them,' Frensen said darkly. 'I could think of one fer instance.'

Christian said nothing. He knew whom the big torpedo-man meant: Von Arco, now squatting below, a seemingly broken man, still shaking as if he were suffering from the plague, no interest in the boat any more. God! What he was going to do with him he just didn't know.

From below came the howls of one of the hydrophone operators who had gone mad. He shrieked invective, crying out at the cruel fate which had done this to him, that had broken his body and his mind.

Christian felt a cold shudder of fear trace its way down the small of his back like an icy finger.

'Louse run over yer liver, Ensign?' Frensen queried.

'Something like that - one with hob-nailed boots,' Christian replied.

Frensen laughed softly. 'That's the way to take it, Ensign. This kind of life we live in the U-Boat Service is too frigging serious to be taken serious. All yer should think of is a bit o' gash, plenty o' suds and schnaps, and have a good laugh now and again. Cos none of us are gonna survive, yer know.'

Christian flashed him a quick glance. The big noncom had spoken in such a matter of fact way as he uttered this overwhelming truth. 'Do you really think so, *Obermaat*?'

'I *know* so, Ensign,' Frensen replied almost cheerfully. 'If we survive this little lot - which is highly doubtful in the opinion of Frau Frensen's handsome son - we won't the next. It's yer law of averages, yer see. Commander Hanssen's time had run out. He's been doing this since the Spanish business. He'd had a good run for his money. It'll be the same with us mark my . . .' He stopped short.

'What is it?'

Frensen didn't answer. Instead he tensed behind the

twin barrels of the anti-aircraft gun, swinging it round with his shoulders.

Christian flung his glasses up. Two fat-bellied flying boats, painted a brilliant white, were coming in low over the water, signal lamps flicking off and on as they signalled to the burning English ship. '*Shit*!' Christian cursed. '*Sunderlands*.'

'Yes, and the friggers are coming straight at us!'

'*Alaaarm . . . alaaarm*!'

Von Arco shot up, hands trembling furiously, eyes darting from side to side as if the enemy might well be inside the U-69 itself. Everywhere the men scrambled through the mess to their duty stations, while Hein, black and dirty, face greased with sweat, called urgently from the control room for more power.

Von Arco pretended not to notice the haste and the running men. When one or the other of them looked at him, he grinned back inanely, as if all were right with the world and this was just another training exercise at which he was merely an observer.

Inside a little voice was telling him to pull himself together. He had already been disgraced in the eyes of these men – he could never serve with them again – but he might still save some of his prestige if he did something now, took an active part in what was happening. But he couldn't. Each time he tried, his body simply refused to obey him. 'Think of what is going to happen when you get back to port,' that cruel little voice within his brain snapped ruthlessly. 'If anyone talks – Hein or Jungblut – you know what it'll mean: a court-martial for cowardice in the face of the enemy. *You've got to act*!'

'But I can't,' von Arco pleaded with the voice. 'I've had enough. My nerves have gone.'

'Well, prepare to take the consequences then, man,' the

little voice persisted sadistically. 'And those are – *death by a firing squad*!'

Von Arco bent his head and began to sob once again, his shoulders heaving like a broken-hearted child.

As he ran by to his duty station, Maydag spat contemptuously into the ankle-deep water at the sobbing von Arco's feet. 'So much for frigging officers and gents!' he sneered. Von Arco did not even hear . . .

'Come on you shitting heroes, do you want to shitting well live for ever?' Frensen hissed as the two Sunderlands grew larger and larger in his ring sight. 'Let's make it quick – *Komm doch*'.

The two four-engined planes broke up. One flew to port; the other to starboard, while Christian watched them anxiously through his binoculars. They took their time. 'Confident bastards,' he hissed to himself. 'They think they've got us and can finish us off at their leisure!'

Frensen seemed to think the same. 'Look at the perverted banana-suckers,' he said through gritted teeth. 'But wait till I put a steel prick up their Tommy arses!'

'*Here they come.*' Christian shrieked.

Abruptly the one flying to port increased speed. The big plane seemed to fall from the sky. Dark round shapes began to fall from its fat belly.

Frensen yelled. He pressed the firing pedal hard. The twin cannon burst into frenetic life. Its song was harsh and staccato but it was music to Christian's ears as the hurrying tracer started to curve lethally towards the Sunderland.

'Left . . . *left*!' Christian yelled furiously. It seemed to him that Frensen was giving too much lead off. But the big, sweating torpedo-man had already realised his mistake. In the same instant that the pattern of exploding bombs began to race across the sea towards them, he adjusted his aim.

The Sunderland staggered visibly as if she had just run into an invisible wall. Suddenly black smoke started to pour from her port engine. She started to come lower and in the very same moment that she swept over the control tower and the bombs exploded all around the U-69 and the world went mad, she simply exploded in mid-air. One moment she was there; the next she was gone and the air was full of great gleaming chunks of aluminium, floating down like a rain of metal leaves.

'*I've got her*! *I've got her*!' Frensen yelled exuberantly as the U-boat reeled back and forth madly in that wild maelstrom. '*Put a prick right up –*'

The rest of his cry of triumph was drowned by the crash of a bomb exploding right on the reserve gun crew, hurrying to take over the forward machine guns. Suddenly they were on fire. Insane human torches, thrashing at their uniforms with hands that were already burning themselves, trying in vain to beat out the flames that engulfed them; flames that ripped at them, tore at them, turning their flesh into a black, bubbling pulp. Some flung themselves overboard in their agony. But the oil from that fire-bomb followed them, slipping into the sea as if it were a live predator not to be cheated of its prey. Others lay on the deck with the tracer ammunition exploding crazily all about them in a lethal fireworks display, their shrinking, charring flesh arching their backs into taut bows, skeleton-arms flung up into a convulsive crucifixion.

Horrified and impotent, Christian tensed at the bridge as a cursing, sweating Frensen peppered the sky with shells after the departing Sunderland. But the fire had saved them; for as the last of those poor men died in agony the plane disappeared on the horizon, leaving them to their fate - either all its bombs gone or satisfied that the U-69 was finished. Soon, Christian told himself furiously, the bastards would be sitting down in their mess to enjoy bacon and eggs, boasting of what they had done, while here he was confronted with a sight that would keep him off eggs and bacon for the rest of his life.

Slowly, painfully, the charred, battered boat limped on, a tiny insignificant speck in that vast, cruel seascape. Could anything save it now?

CHAPTER 7

The fat engineer-officer Hein stared helplessly at the cold, grey, drifting fog. 'The men are beat, Jungblut. At the end of their tethers.' He shrugged hopelessly and Christian could see just how weary he was. 'The shitting engines have let me down. I can't coax more than eight knots out of them on the surface.'

'And underwater – what about the electric motors?' Christian forced himself to sound purposeful, remembering the way Hanssen had always kept control of hopeless situations.

'*Shot*! The last bomb did for the batteries. There's nothing for it. We've got to stick it out on the surface.'

'I've signalled Kiel. They know we're coming,' Christian said. 'When we reach our own coastal waters they'll be waiting to escort us in. Twelve hours or so and we will have done it.'

'*If*!' Von Arco broke his long silence, sounding rational for the first time since he had broken down.

Christian turned to him slowly. Now he could understand the strains and stresses of combat, but he would rather have died than given way to his cowardice in the disgraceful manner von Arco had. It took an effort of will now to hide his contempt as he spoke. 'How do you mean, *Herr Oberleutnant*?' he asked.

'No one in his right mind would attempt to get the U-69 back to base,' von Arco snapped with a trace of his old arrogance, though the fear was still clear in his red-rimmed eyes. 'The crew are out on their feet - what's left of them. We have no defence save the twin AA cannon and our motors are crippled. Don't you agree, Hein?'

The engineer shrugged his shoulders helplessly and said nothing.

'And what do you suggest we do, *Herr Oberleutnant*?' Christian rasped, emphasizing the rank contemptuously.

'What do you think? Surrender! That's obvious, isn't it? Once the Tommies spot us again they'll send us to the bottom without mercy, any fool knows that. After the business in Scapa and what has occurred since, do you think they are going to show any mercy on us?' Von Arco gulped hard as if he had just realized the full implications of his own words. '*Surrender*!' he repeated. 'That's the only answer.'

Christian looked at him, truly shocked. 'You can't mean that?' he stuttered. He looked wildly at Hein, but the fat engineer kept his head down, as if he wanted no part in the discussion. Christian realised to his horror that Hein had lost his will to resist too; he would go along with any decision that was made. 'There's hope, von Arco. One can't give up without a fight, man!'

'There is absolutely no hope, you silly young fool. We've had it and the sooner we hoist the white flag the better.' Von Arco grinned sardonically. 'My God, Jungblut, learn the facts of life. We're finished! The crew knows it too. They'd be only too happy to throw in the white towel at this very moment.'

Christian listened aghast. Was he really listening to a convinced National Socialist and a German naval officer speaking? For a moment he was lost. Here he was at twenty, and von Arco and Hein were senior officers, five or six years older than he; perhaps they were right, being mature and realistic about the terrible situation in which they found themselves. Besides he was not even a fully commissioned officer, only an ensign: neither fish nor fowl. *What was he to do?*

At that moment Christian Jungblut – though he did not know it – was faced with the most momentous decision of his whole career in the *Kriegsmarine*. It was a decision that would change him from a callow youth to the man who would become one of Germany's greatest submarine aces. But if anyone had asked him at that moment why he decided the way he did, he would not have been able to answer readily. 'Duty', he might have said. But what was duty? It was his father, the long line of bemedalled veterans on *Heldengedenktag** and the even longer line of cripples in their wheeled wickerwork baskets and invalid carriages who followed them. It was the crisp stamp of the cadets' boots on gravel, the bugle calls, the hoisting of the flag, the hoarse choruses of the *Deutschlandlied* – the feeling of belonging to something which was more important than oneself. It was that ill-defined feeling – more a kind of spiritual warmth – which made a young man believe that it was worth sacrificing one's life for it. It was something which one had to do – without question.

Thus it was that when he spoke again his young voice was confident and his tired eyes were full of hope: 'I shall talk to the men, von Arco.'

'You just do that,' von Arco sneered.

Christian ignored him. 'Hein,' he commanded, 'you take over the conn while I go below.'

'Yes sir,' Hein said automatically, responding to the note of authority in Christian's voice. Suddenly he flushed as he realised that he had addressed an ensign as 'sir'. Von Arco's sneer grew even larger.

Hastily Christian clattered down the dripping ladder into the littered confusion of the U-69. The place was in a

* 'Memory of Heroes' Day' – the German Equivalent of 'Armistice Day'

terrible shambles. Oil and water slopped about. A bag of flour had burst open. Tins rolled back and forth like clockwork toys. Christian noted the mess automatically as he faced the crew. For a moment he hated the sight of them and their stupid, silent faces. Why didn't they do something about the mess? Why did they simply slump there, accepting the inevitable like a lot of dumb cattle waiting for the slaughter to come? His temper flared up. He would have dearly loved to round on them: hadn't he tried hard enough – the youngest member of the crew? Hadn't he taken over when von Arco had broken down? Wasn't he still damnwell trying?

Instead he said calmly and slowly, as if he were speaking to some particular slow and none-too-intelligent elderly people, 'They're expecting us in Kiel. They'll send out surface craft to protect us. There's only ten hours of daylight left.' He forced a winning smile though he had never felt less like smiling. 'We're almost back – home to mother!'

There was no response. They remained slumped there, mute and beaten.

Christian forced himself to relax, unclench his fists, drop his aggressive hunch. 'Now I suggest all of you not on duty set about cleaning up this mess. We're swimming in the shit. Who knows,' he quipped, 'the Big Lion himself might *personally* come and pay us a visit, bringing the usual goodies. We wouldn't like the Big Lion to think that the U-69 was an untidy boat, would we?'

'Have we got a chance, Ensign?' one of the younger ratings asked softly. He swayed suddenly. A comrade grabbed him. He was bleeding from a gash across the temple, both his hands were crooked into charred claws with severe burns, and the look in his eyes verged on madness.

Christian swallowed hard. What was he going to say? The kid hadn't a hope. The shock was killing him – even he could see that. By the time they got him back to the naval hospital in Kiel – if they ever did manage that – he would be dead. The kid was dying on his feet.

'Of course we'll frigging well get back!' a determined Hamburg voice growled in the accents of the waterfront. Christian looked up. Frensen stood there at the hatch leading to the torpedo room, a dirty, bloodstained bandage wrapped round his head where he had been struck by shrapnel while operating the AA cannon. He winked at Christian. 'What's the matter with you lot? Ain't we the muff-lovers of the old sixty-nine? We've had a bit of bad luck, a bit o' stick, but we've had worse, shipmates. Now come on, do as the Ensign says.' He aimed a kick at a tin on the floor and sent it flying as if to emphasise his words and suddenly they were moving; not with any speed that was for sure, but they *were* moving, taking hold of shovels and brooms, cursing furiously as they did so.

Christian gave a little sigh. 'When you've cleared up the gash,' he ordered, 'the cook can make some "nigger sweat" and break out some canned fruit.'

That brought a mutter of appreciation. They all liked the sweet syrup of the canned fruit. 'Thank you, sir,' someone said and Christian felt himself flush with pleasure. Twice now he had been called 'sir'. It was a heady feeling for a twenty-year-old ensign. He clattered up the ladder to the bridge smartly as if he really were the Skipper of the U-69. Behind him his 'muff-lovers' worked with a will . . .

Five hundred miles away, as the sirens wailed their dread warning Churchill snapped angrily at Payne, 'Well, now we know that one of the buggers has reached Germany – this fellow Prien of theirs.' He slapped the message transcript. 'Doctor Goebbels is having a field-day with him. The man who sank the *Royal Oak*!' Churchill snorted and took an angry drag at his big cigar.

Outside the air-raid wardens were shrilling their whistles and someone was running down the street turning a rattle. 'Don't yer know there's a war on?' an angry voice was shouting.

'One piece of good news, sir,' Payne said. 'Coastal Command has just reported that one of their Sunderlands attacked, set on fire and probably sank a U-boat heading on a south-easterly course - obviously on its way back to Germany.'

Churchill nodded his approval. 'Well, that's something to give the press tonight. But there were three, weren't there?'

'Yessir.'

'So there must be one left at sea.' He considered for a moment as outside the sirens died away, leaving behind a loud-echoing silence. Payne stared nervously through the window at the grey sky. He wished Churchill would release him so he could go to the shelter. Whitehall was an obvious target for German bombers but Churchill never seemed to care. Sometimes it was almost as if he wished to die 'in battle', as he called it, though for the life of him he could not see what was so very glorious about having your head blown off by a bomb.

'The Fifth Flotilla is in position by now, Payne?' Churchill asked.

'Yessir. Flag officer Harwich reports that they are in position to block the entrance to the Baltic and to the North Sea Canal for the next forty-eight hours. Coastal Command is providing air cover.'

'Excellent.' Suddenly Churchill slammed his chubby fist down on his desk, making Payne jump. 'I want the other bugger, Payne! Those poor chaps on the dear old *Royal Oak* have to be avenged. *I want that last submarine destroyed*! Is that understood?'

'Yessir,' Payne answered.

'Then get on with it!' Churchill growled.

Payne fled to the shelters, leaving Churchill slumped at his desk, the rumble of guns and the snarl of airplane engines unheard, that black feeling of despair he knew so well beginning to overcome him. Eight hundred of his tars had died, without a shot in their defence having been fired. They had to be avenged. Slowly two large tears began to trickle down the old man's face . . .

CHAPTER 8

The last of the dead crewmen, each sewn up in white canvas, slid over the side of the battered U-69. Christian saluted formally and stood there for a moment as if in silent prayer. On the bridge above him, von Arco seemed totally unconcerned about the dead submariners. His gaze was concentrated exclusively on the grey wall of fog ahead and he was beginning to tremble again.

He had not said a word when Christian had reported to Hein the crew's reaction to his exhortations. But when Hein had responded with new-found energy, 'Well then, we'll do it after all, Jungblut,' von Arco had exploded: 'You're mad, man! *Totally mad*! We haven't got a chance – and you damnwell know it!'

Christian had ignored him. Still he had not felt that he possessed sufficient authority to order him off the bridge. So there von Arco stood; an unwanted look-out obviously intent on saving his own skin if they bumped into trouble. Christian turned away. Now he concentrated on having another machine gun set up aft, as the U-69 limped eastwards at a snail's pace.

'Popguns!' Maydag, who was to man it, growled. 'Two MGs and a twenty millimetre flak gun against the whole of the English navy!'

Christian forced a grin: 'You've heard of David and Goliath, haven't you?'

'Nope,' Maydag answered. 'Never go in fer that kind of

stuff, Ensign. Reading softens yer brain. Besides, it takes yer mind off gash.'

Christian shook his head in mock wonder and then, satisfied that his defences were the best he could make them, he returned to the bridge and took his post, eyes narrowed to slits against the damp, clinging fog.

There were about five hours left now till darkness would fall and they could reach the German coast. If this fog held up till then they stood a good chance of getting through. Suddenly Christian felt completely confident and in control. Of course they'd get through. His 'muff-eaters' had suffered enough. He was going to save them!

The red flare spurted up through the grey fog with startling suddenness. Christian reacted immediately, as next to him von Arco gasped with fear, 'Prepare for action, gun crews! Stand by there now!'

He tensed, staring hard to port as the flare spluttered and hissed and began to drop like a fallen angel, leaving behind a tense, brooding silence, broken only by the steady throb of the U-69's diesels.

'Could it be ours?' Hein called up anxiously from below.

Christian shook his head. 'Doubt it. They would have attempted a recognition signal if they were. No,' he said grimly, 'that's definitely the Royal Navy and they're out looking for us.' Swiftly he rapped out a new course and the crippled boat began to limp towards a cloud of thicker fog, while Christian, his fists clenched tensely, stared hard at the grey wall in front of him, waiting expectantly for the inevitable.

Suddenly there was the Tommy. The roar of its engines was ear-splitting as the motor torpedo-boat came hurtling out of the fog bow-high, wild, white water spurting up on both sides as it cleaved its way through the waves. Maydag didn't wait for an order. He opened up immediately.

Tracer zipped lethally towards the MTB. Next to Christian the AA-gunner depressed his weapon furiously, trying to engage the enemy, while von Arco cowered behind the protection of the conning-tower.

The MTB's first torpedo hissed into the water, followed a second later by another. For an instant Christian could see the twin arrows of white racing straight for the U-69. '*HARD TO PORT*!' he yelled desperately.

Down below, Hein reacted immediately, his fat face scarlet with the effort. Slowly, desperately slowly, the U-69 started to swing round. Christian gripped the rail with white-knuckled hands, body tensed for the tremendous impact to come. But again luck was on their side. First one, then the other torpedo flashed by them in a flurry of furious white bubbles. Next moment the MTB was swinging round in a tremendous white, boiling curve of water, followed by Maydag's tracer bullets.

'Surrender!' von Arco cried, voice choked with emotion. 'Surrender, for God's sake . . . we haven't got a chance!'

Christian ignored him. 'All right, gunner, are you ready?' he yelled at the man at the AA cannon.

'Yes sir.'

'Prepare for another attack. Try to get her bridge –'

'Here she comes again, sir!' Maydag screamed from the deck below.

'*FEUER*!' Christian cried.

The gunner hit the firing button with his foot. The long-barrelled 20mm cannon burst into crazy, pulsating life. A wall of hurrying white sped towards the MTB.

Christian threw up his glasses. The MTB slid knife-like onto the circles of calibrated glass. A great white wave shot up from her bows as she cleaved the water at fifty kilometres an hour. He caught a glimpse of a pale young face under a jauntily tilted white cap on the bridge: her Skipper.

The cannon pounded crazily. The white shells riveted a

line across her bows. A man fell, arms waving crazily, over the side. Her superstructure started to disappear, a mess of whirling bits of metal and wood. The bridge and the Skipper were swept away and then she was sweeping by in a flood of water, her guns raking the U-69.

Shell fragments and tracer hissed everywhere lethally. Next to Christian one of the look-outs screamed shrilly and slumped to the deck, carrying von Arco with him, blood jetting in a bright-scarlet arc from his throat. He died groaning horribly, drowning slowly in his own blood. Something hit Christian in the head – hard. He brushed it away as if it were some irritating fly and his hand came back wet and sticky with blood. Below, Hein shouted then dropped as if pole-axed, the back of his head a red mess. He was dead before he hit the deck.

Christian pushed away the gunner who was lying dead across the cannon, while below the Chief Petty Officer rushed to take over the conn from the dead engineer-officer. Below, one of the dying crew fought off death violently: '*Whoresons . . . pigs, you can't do this to me . . . bleeding arseholes, it ain't fair . . . Leave me alone . .* !'

Christian waited, the blood dripping steadily from his wounded head, eyes searching the fog for the next appearance of the MTB. They were English. They wouldn't give in easily. They'd come back all right.

'*There's the bastard*!' Maydag yelled and started firing immediately.

Christian gasped and swung his cannon round. A bit slower now, dragging her shattered superstructure through the water, the Tommy was charging straight in for the kill! '*Take this*!' Christian cried, as down below the dying man gave up the ghost with one last 'frigging unfair'. He pressed the foot bar. The twin cannon leapt into action. He could feel the satisfying *thwack-thwack* of the pounding cannon smacking into his shoulder as shells raced towards the MTB at a rate of one thousand rounds a minute.

Still the English came on while great pieces of metal and wood were ripped from its hull by that tremendous barrage. Now the English were firing too and the U-69 reeled and heeled under the shock of shells exploding all around her. Grimly Christian hung on as the shells rushed through the air like locomotives through a tunnel, deafening him, sucking the very air out of his lungs so that in a flash he was gasping like an asthmatic.

Now the MTB blotted out the whole horizon. It towered above the sub. 'The brave, silly bastards!' Christian gasped as Maydag wheeled round, clutching his suddenly shattered shoulder, bright-red blood suddenly seeping through his tightly clenched fingers. '*They're gonna ram us*!'

Suddenly, with all the terrible finality of a nightmare, he realised that was just what the English were going to do. The didn't care whether they lived or died. But if they were to die, they were going to have the satisfaction of taking the German down with them.

'Hein!' he called desperately. 'Hard to . . .' He looked down and stopped short. Hein was dead. 'Chief Petty Officer!' he cried in near-despair. 'Swing her round! The Tommies are going to ram –'

The burst of machine gun fire caught him in the shoulder with a blow like a sledgehammer. He staggered away from the cannon not feeling the pain one bit, though his right arm hung now by shreds of scarlet flesh specked with the brilliant gleaming white of broken bone fragments.

'Help,' he gasped as that terrible avenging MTB, half its crew dead or dying, raced ever closer. 'Paula, help me!' he sighed, only aware of the great roaring darkness that threatened to overwhelm him at any moment and the wrecked boat, the tattered white ensign hanging limply from its shattered stern as it roared towards the sub. 'Paula!' he gasped, swaying violently like a drunk.

Now the two boats were bound on a collision course. There was no way out, they were going to slam into each other. The guns had ceased firing. There was no sound save that of engines.

'*Paula!*'

The lean grey shape sliced out of the fog. At its stern fluttered proudly the black and white flag of the German *Kriegsmarine*. The bow guns thundered into life. The MTB boat reared right out of the sea, her screws churning impotently. With startling abruptness she disintegrated. Her oil tanks exploded in a searing eruption of purple flame. Christian felt the shock of that tremendous explosion as if a gigantic fist had just squeezed his guts. His eyes were closing. He tried to open them but couldn't. 'Paula,' he sighed one more time as the MTB's stern, consumed by a monstrous funeral pyre, started to slide into the hissing, spluttering sea. He too began to fall to the holed and debris-littered bridge of the U-69. It was all over . . .

Envoi

'There are no roses on a sailor's grave,
No lilies on an ocean wave.
The only tribute is the seagulls' sweeps
And the teardrops that a sweetheart weeps.'

Old German sailors' song

Leutnant zur See Christian Jungblut walked slowly down the street where she had lived, boots crunching on the remains of the glass from the windows the mob must have smashed. The window of the grocer she had comforted had been long boarded up and the place left deserted; just like those of the cellar where they had made love that last night.

'Gone, *Herr Leutnant*,' the skinny little postman had informed him moments before, from behind a hand held to his mouth. 'One day they were there - the Yids I mean - the next they were gone.' He had lowered his voice and whispered, '*Nacht und Nebel** if you ask me, Lieutenant.'

Now the street was empty of its Jews and Paula Petersen had vanished just as surely as had Commander Hanssen, the fat little engineer and all the rest. They had all been involved in battle one way or another. Christian walked on reflectively, automatically saluting the ratings, who were everywhere, with an arm that still ached. 'Sharks and little fishes,' he told himself sadly; and once again the 'sharks' had won. When would it ever end?

Six hours before he had reported for duty in Kiel in order to receive his new posting, now that the bone-menders had certified he was fit for active duty again. There another of the 'sharks' had been waiting for him: no less a person than the latest 'naval hero', Lt. Commander

* 'Night and fog': the usual name given for a covert night arrest by the Gestapo

von Arco now, on Doenitz' staff and wearing the Knight's Cross he had won for having brought the crippled U-69 back to port so bravely after all her officers had been killed.

'You will report immediately to the U-69 in Hamburg, Jungblut,' he had snapped, obviously his old arrogant self again, though Christian had noted that he avoided looking at him directly.

Christian had stared at him coldly. There had been no witnesses to his cowardice (save for the ratings) and once that destroyer had knocked out the Tommy MTB and there had been no more danger von Arco had recovered and had brought the boat in. Everyone had accepted his own account of his 'heroism' and Dr Goebbels* had made much of it. The papers had fussed for days about the brave, selfless Lt. von Arco. The Führer himself had personally presented the newly promoted Lt. Commander von Arco with his medal at Berchtesgaden. Now he had achieved what he had wanted all along: glory and a safe staff job. He had become a 'rear-echelon stallion'; he would survive the war.

He had handed Christian his orders, looked at the latter's new Iron Cross and had opened his mouth as if he had wanted to say some more. Christian had not given him the chance. Curtly he had barked, 'Thank you,' omitting the 'sir'. Without a salute he had turned and marched out, leaving von Arco to stare at his back, the arrogant expression on his face replaced by worry. The sooner Jungblut went back to sea and got himself killed in action, he told himself, the better it would be for him. From now onwards Christian Jungblut represented a permanent threat – for he knew the truth. *Jungblut had to die – and die soon . . .*

Slowly and reflectively Christian walked on down to the docks where the U-69 was being refitted. It was growing

* German Minister of Propaganda

dark already. Soon they'd be putting up the black-outs; and in the seamen's haunts, loud with drunken laughter and the tinny squawk of accordion music, the fat innkeepers with their inevitable cigars were drawing the thick felt curtains. Another wartime night was beginning to descend upon the waterfront. Christian allowed himself a faint smile. The men were enjoying their time out of war. But soon the war would open up its greedy maws again and attempt to swallow them up; they deserved their rough and ready fun.

> '*Should we sink to the ocean floor*
> *We still shall walk to the nearest*
> *shore*,' that old familiar boozy voice
> bellowed raucously. 'To *you, Lili Marlene,*
> *to you, Lili Marlene.*'

Christian swung round.

There was no mistaking those enormous shoulders and broad, brick-red face. It was *Obermaat* Frensen and his running-mate Maydag, the former carrying a huge salami sausage, as long and thick as his arm; the latter a bottle of seaman's rum. They saw him in the very same instant that he spotted them. They stiffened to attention and solemnly Frensen presented arms with the huge sausage. 'Welcome home, sir,' he boomed, and there was no mistaking the warmth in his thick waterfront voice.

Christian touched his hand to his cap in salute too and said, 'Thank you, *Obermaat*. Well then, don't just stand there like a fart waiting to hit the side of the thunderbox! Let's get on home before it's too dark!'

Chatting animatedly like the old comrades they were, comrades who had not seen each other for a long long time, they hurried down the mean, cobbled street to where she waited for them: that lean, grey, deadly shape which was their home - the U-69. They were going to war again . . .